Praise

CW01476977

"*The Question* is
like a diamond. Her
insights, to enchant you into wisdom."
—**Tim Freke,** author of *Soul Story, How Long is Now?,* and many other books

"Elyn Aviva's own courageous and experiential explorations of the nature of reality and its foundational imaginal realms are brought to vivid life and with wisdom and lyric beauty in this wonder-full allegory.
—**Dr Jude Currivan,** cosmologist and author of *The Cosmic Hologram: In-formation at the Center of Creation*

"I am not a reader of fantasy, but Elyn Aviva's narrative is so compelling and mystically appealing that it pulled me in. She has such a magical way of weaving character and plot, incident and esoteric information that it's like entering virtual reality. Start the first page and you won't take off the viewing goggles till the last sentence."
—**Judith Fein,** author of *Life Is a Trip: The Transformative Magic of Travel* and *The Spoon from Minkowitz*

"In Elyn Aviva's 'maybe fiction' *The Question* we start our journey on the Main Street of real dreamers, the path of moonlight on water. We have so many stories to hear. Some of them come with names from old mythologies, like Gwydion and Cerberus and Isis, but they shapeshift and shake out their feathers, reminding us that a myth to live by must be dyed with our own passion and imagination and cut to our lifestyle. Sometimes it feels like we have wandered into a tarot novella like Italo Calvino's *The Castle of Crossed Destinies*. Then we realize that the cards in play don't come from any familiar deck but are swooping down from the imaginal realm to carry us into adventures there. We learn that the most important questions can't merely be answered; they must be lived. *The Question* animates one of my favorite themes: that we live by stories and must seek to find and live our bigger and braver stories and tell them so well that we entertain Death and earn the right kind of time in this world."

—**Robert Moss,** creator of Active Dreaming, bestselling author of *Conscious Dreaming, The Secret History of Dreaming*, and *The Boy Who Died and Came Back*

"In this fable Elyn Aviva explores the life and afterlife of the soul."

—**Patrice Chaplin,** author and playwright, including *City of Secrets* and *The Stone Cradle*

"I love the wisdom and depth in this new book! This will be a valuable tool for many. Multi-layered dimensions of reality, cleverly pieced together, and definitely for the intelligent reader."

—**Ani Williams,** musician and author

"Elyn Aviva has spent many years studying esoteric and magical subjects. She brings this knowledge forward to inform and underpin her fiction writing. This novel abounds with mysterious characters and transformative magical forces, in a flurry of encounters and challenging interactions."

—**R J Stewart,** composer, author, and teacher

THE QUESTION

A magical fable

THE QUESTION

A *magical fable*

Elyn Aviva

To Tim —
An inspiring teacher with a
BIG heart! Your work is deeply
fundamental to this book &
I thank you for it.
Blessings &
"Big" love —
Elyn

Interior and cover design by Gary White.

Trattatello font © 2005 James Grieshaber. All rights reserved.

THE QUESTION

A Magical Fable

by

Elyn Aviva

Copyright © 2018 by Pilgrims Process Publishers

ISBN: 978-0-9915267-6-5

Library of Congress Control Number:

2018941142

Printed in the United States of America

Acknowledgements

I want to give my deep thanks and appreciation to three teachers I have studied with over the years: R.J. Stewart, Tim Freke, and Robert Moss. R.J.'s Inner Temples/Inner Convocation workshops and *Living Magical Arts* and *Sphere of Art* books have given me the experiential background in the Western esoteric tradition that underlies this story. Tim's paralogical, both/and philosophy and his ideas about the nature of time and the soul weave their way through *The Question*. Master storyteller Robert Moss's Active Dreamwork infuses this manuscript. His Lightning Dreamwork process includes responding to someone else's dream with, "If this were my dream …." I also want to thank Judie Fein, an inspiring travel writer and my writing mentor. She has helped me to learn how to tell a story.

And last but always first in my heart, my beloved partner/spouse/best friend, Gary White, who has been with me throughout this journey and provided valuable, trustworthy advice and enormous logistic and emotional support.

✳

Reader's Note: References and word associations are provided at the end of the story (pages 178-184). The Index begins on page 185.

One

The full moon floats over the tranquil lake, admiring her own reflection gleaming as bright as a fresh-minted silver coin. As I stroll along the sandy shore, I pick up a stone and toss it into the still waters. Abruptly the mirrored moon shatters into dancing slivers of light.

The string of broken moonbeams follows me like a compass needle as I amble along. When I was young, I followed that path of shimmering sparks up to the moon. I wonder: Could I make that journey now? As if to answer, the moon coyly hides behind a passing cloud, and the moon-lit path abruptly disappears.

The water-soaked sand barely sinks beneath my feet. I look behind me. Water is slowly, inevitably welling up into my footprints, gradually blurring their shape. Soon all traces of the path I have made behind me will disappear. Ahead of me there is only smooth, unmarked sand.

I feel a growing sense of urgency. It's time to tell my story. But who will listen? And who will have ears to hear?

The moon has recovered from her momentary bashfulness and is once again admiring her reflection in the glassy surface of the lake. I smile at her buoyant lunacy. She seems to smile back.

I hear the nearby trees rustle in the breeze and a faint whisper: "When the time is right, the right listener will appear."

And then I hear another sound, not much louder than an echo. A voice calls out to me, "Tell me a story!"

I look around. Someone is sitting on a nearby dune, watching me. He looks vaguely familiar, but in the moonlight I can't quite recognize who he is. A distant relative? A long-lost friend?

Perhaps he is a faithful student, sent to watch over my frail and failing self. For I am old now and preparing to meet Death, my death, my sometime enemy, my frequent companion. I am preparing to pass on, or over. Preparing in life for life after death—or life after life. What you call it doesn't really matter, but what and how you think about it is of immense importance.

The figure on the dune calls out again. "Tell me a story!" He gestures widely with his stumpy arms, urging me to approach.

I walk back to the dune and sit down next to him on the sand. I look at him, up close in the moonlight, but moonlight is a light that conceals as much as it reveals, that reflects as much as it distorts. His head seems a bit misshapen, his ears unnaturally large, his nose pendulous. I almost recognize him, but not quite.

He tilts his head and waits, expectantly.

I make my decision. "I will tell you a story, my story, but it will be a long one—long enough to last through the setting of the moon and the rising of the sun. Long enough—but no longer than is necessary. Are you willing to hear it? Are you ready to listen?"

He nods eagerly and pulls things out of his surprisingly copious leather knapsack. A thermos of steaming chai, which he offers to me, a blanket, which he spreads out beside me, a notebook, and an ivory pen. He opens the notebook on his ample lap and prepares to write. He licks the sharp pen nib, and the ink seems to flow red onto the unlined page as he inscribes the date. Perhaps it is just an illusion of the moonlight.

"Ready when you are," he replies, sitting cross-legged, leaning his back against the dune.

3

I, too, lean back against the dune. I nod and begin.

✳

Many years ago, I was going through a very difficult time. Now I can smile about it, but at that time, life had lost its meaning. I had lost my way. I didn't know what to do or, equally important, what not to do. Distraught, I found myself wandering through an ancient city, successfully losing myself in its maze of twisting lanes and narrow alleys. Of course, I had already gone astray, so losing myself was an easy thing to do.

By chance I peered into the grimy window of a used book store. A faded advertisement pasted in one corner caught my eye. In bold letters it announced: *"Feeling lost? Help is near. In fact, it's here. First reading, free."* I wondered what kind of reading was being offered: Palm reading? Tarot cards? Some sort of runes? Although I was skeptical by nature, I was desperate and ready to try anything.

I turned the worn brass handle and pushed open the creaky wooden door. An old-fashioned bell attached to the door-hinge tinkled as I walked in. The tiny room smelled musty and slightly mildewed. In the dust-filled light, I saw walls lined with overflowing bookshelves and tables covered with collapsing stacks of tattered magazines. Rolled prints and papyrus scrolls poked out of a cracked vase on the floor.

Hand-written shelf-labels indicated an effort had once been made to organize the collection into categories: "False Philosophy," "Esoterica," "Exotica," "Outer Space Travel," "Inner Space Travel," "Non-fiction Maybe," "Maybe Fiction," "Never to Be Read Aloud." I smiled. It appeared the shop owner had a sense of humor. Other labels were written in some kind of hieroglyphics and in languages I had never seen before. Dimly lit hallways led off in different directions.

"Hello? Anyone here?" I called out. There was no answer, though I thought I heard a faint rustling in a corner. Rats, I wondered, or perhaps a resident cat?

Just as I was about to leave, I saw a light go on behind a narrow, ill-fitted door that looked like it opened into a closet. A sign hanging on the door stated, "Open for business."

I knocked.

A throaty voice called out, "Come in."

I entered and look around. The room was surprisingly large, as if the space had somehow expanded beyond the confines of the shop.

A woman sat on a clear, Plexiglas chair at a round, mirror-top table. She gestured to the empty chair across from her, and I sat down nervously.

She began drawing cards out of the air with her long, slim fingers. The Tarot Magician trump appeared, then a wolf spirit-guide card, followed by a colorful Kabbalist Tree of Life diagram.

She glanced at me and asked rhetorically, "Why be limited to working with only one deck of cards?"

I watched, mesmerized.

She raised her left hand again and, with a curious spiraling twist of her fingers, another card appeared and floated gently down through the air. The table-top was soon covered with a kaleidoscope of cards of different designs, shapes, and sizes. She stirred the mirage with both hands and then looked at me, her glance piercing me like a rook's.

"Now, what is your question?"

I took a deep breath and prepared to speak.

She raised an imperious hand. "You don't have to tell me."

I nodded silently. A clock ticked in the background, then stopped. I turned to find the source of sound but there was none. The walls were bare. Bare and lit as if with moonlight.

"In case you were wondering, the time is always now," the Seer declared and laughed a laugh that tinkled like a bell. Then she shook herself, as if shaking off a chill. "Let's begin. Pick your first card."

"Wait—" I protested, as if suddenly coming out of a spell. "Wait! Who are you? What is this place?"

She laughed, this time an odd, barking laugh. "Is that your question? Your *real* question? I think not. Let's begin. Time is a-wasting, although there is no time. And opportunity is wasting as well. You may not get another chance. Pick your first card."

6

I reached toward the multitude of cards. One card moved toward my outstretched hand as if drawn by an unseen attraction. I gave it to her. She turned it over. I saw a raven, a stream, a dead man.

"If I were you, and this were *my* card," she began....

Playing the Raven Card

The raven pecks eagerly at the left eye of the dead person lying in the stream. The corpse's legs straddle the bank; its head rocks to and fro in the gently moving waters. Dampness seeps down its pants, darkening them from dirty tan to dark brown. Blood tinges the murky green water with arabesque tendrils, shading from red to faded pink.

I smell the sharp scent of blood in the air and taste it like rust on my tongue.

My boots crunch on the stubble of dry grass on the riverbank. The large black bird with its large black beak turns to look at me, startled at my approach. With a harsh "Kraa" it flies up, its long-fingered wings beating sonorously, lifting its weight quickly with each powerful thrust. The raven flies across the stream. A tail feather floats down and lands on my left foot. I look down. I look up. The raven has disappeared.

A tall, slender figure appears. I think it is a woman, but I can't see her face because she is veiled. She is shrouded in white gauzy fabric wrapped around her like a winding cloth. Blood spatters her hem.

7

I feel compelled to cross the stream to the Other Side. I must meet the woman and find the raven. I look both ways. There is no bridge in sight. I realize there is no way around: the only way is through. In the distance, a ferryman approaches, accompanied by a slavering three-headed dog with a snake-like tail, snarling and snapping as it runs back and forth in the narrow, rocking skiff.

Better to take my chances in the stream, I decide, rather than risk riding on that boat. Besides, my pockets are empty, so I have no coin with which to pay the ferryman.

I prepare for full-body baptism. I stuff my socks in my boots, tie the laces together, and drape them across my shoulders. Then I step off the grassy bank into unexpected frigidity. I wade in deeper, and soft, gooey mud sucks at my feet. Fish nibble between my legs, and slimy underwater weeds twine around my waist as I half-slide, half-glide my feet across the streambed.

Suddenly the bottom drops away and I sink beneath the surface. Sputtering with shock and cold, I struggle not to breathe the muck-stirred waters and frantically push myself back up from below, grabbing my boots as they drift away. I begin to dogpaddle across, occasionally bobbing down with my outstretched toes to test the depth. Soon I encounter jagged rocks and rounded pebbles, and I start to walk through water once again.

I reach the far bank, teeth chattering, and drag myself ashore, dripping from head to toes.

The veiled figure nods in approval; the raven perched on her shoulder turns its head and whispers in her ear. She nods again.

Still barefoot, I approach cautiously and with respect.

"You have passed the first test," she says in a croaking voice. The movement of her breath causes her finely woven veil to flutter in and out. A faint scent of spikenard and myrrh escapes with every exhalation.

The raven extends its wings and flies over to me, grasping my right shoulder with its dirty black talons. The pain is intense. It "Kraa's" loudly in my ear and slightly loosens its grip. I look at the raven, gasping at the stench of decay that permeates its breath. The odor is inevitable, since the carrion-eater is an active participant in the cycle of life and death. I turn back to speak to the woman in white, but she has disappeared.

The Seer—for so I had named her—dropped the card into the assortment reflected in the mirrored tabletop. My right shoulder hurt, as if my muscles had been clenched or something had been clenching it. I rubbed it with my left hand.

Frowning, I said, "That was a most unusual reading. In fact, I've never had a card reading like it. Not that I've had many readings."

She looked at me with piercing, raven-black eyes. "I'm not like other Seers."

"I see that now." I paused, trying to think of what to say, but at a loss for words.

She tapped her black stiletto heels against the floor. Her black purse swayed gently from the back of the Plexiglas chair. "If you have any doubts, now is the time to leave."

Words came at last, and I blurted out again, "Who *are* you? What *is* this place?"

She ignored my questions. "Are you ready to continue?"

"Not yet!" I repeated urgently, "Who *are* you?"

"I suppose you think that matters. It doesn't. Who are *you*? Do you really know? Who you are now is not who you were yesterday. You can be sure of that. And who you are today will not be who you are tomorrow. You can be sure of that as well."

She sighed, and her breath smelled like wild honey and lavender. Then she spread her hands in the air over the tabletop. "You have been called here to answer your deepest question. Don't squander this unique opportunity on trivia."

Suddenly I remembered an old fairytale in which the hero was given three wishes and frittered them away. I was determined not to make that mistake. I had no idea what was happening, but maybe I didn't need to understand, at least not yet.

"Well then." I cleared my throat. "About the cards. About the reading you just did. I want you to tell me more. I want you to tell me what the card means."

She began to stir the cards, her vermillion lips twisting in a lopsided smile. "What does the card mean?

What do *you* think it means? It's *your* card, after all. You drew the card, not me. However, I can tell you who some of the characters are or might have been: Charon, the Ferryman who takes people across the River Styx, and his dog, Cerberus; the psychopomp Raven; the Morrigan—but these are just labels. You must make the story your own."

I didn't know how to respond, so I asked another question. "What did the veiled woman mean when she said, 'you passed the first test'? How many tests are there?"

The Seer continued to stare at the reflections on the table. "'Some things are not meant to be understood by the mind but must be grasped by the soul.'"

I was increasingly confused. "What is it that you see? The future?" I asked.

"There is no future. There is only possibility."

"But what about the past?"

"The past accumulates. Don't you feel its weight pushing against you, pressing you against the permeable membrane of Now? On the other side of Now lies the infinite, ever-expanding realm of the possible."

Puzzled, I replied, "So there is a past—or 'the' past—even if there's no future?"

"Of course. The past doesn't just disappear. Think about it: where would it go? It is always here, accumulating. Moreover, the past becomes present when we think about it."

11

Cautiously, I said, "Given the advertisement on the window, I assumed you were a kind of fortune teller. Doesn't that mean you tell the future?"

She scowled. "Assumptions are dangerous. They prepare you to expect the wrong thing and blind you to what is actually happening." She continued in a calmer tone, "Let me begin by clearing up a misunderstanding. I am not a fortune teller. I am a Seer. I read the story I see hidden in the cards. To quote a master storyteller, 'Each of us is living a story. If we don't know that, we may be living the wrong story, a small and confining story wound around us by other people's beliefs and expectations.'"

She pointed to the table. "Mix the cards and choose one."

Again a card seemed drawn to my outstretched hand. I gave it to the Seer and she turned it over. It was a painting of a bedraggled, bronze-feathered bird perched in a tree.

"What kind of bird do you think you see?" she asked.

I looked closely. "Maybe a merlin. Or a peregrine falcon? Or a Maltese falcon, in disguise?"

She smiled with amusement and ran her red-tipped fingers through her thick, raven-black hair. "You don't know much about birds, do you?"

"Could it be a gyrfalcon?" I asked, grasping at the echo of a memory.

She recited in a sing-song voice, "'Turning and turning in the widening gyre/ The falcon cannot hear the falconer;/ Things fall apart; the center cannot hold...' The opening lines of W.B. Yeats' brilliant poem, 'The Second Coming.' Good try, and perhaps relevant to the card, but no, that's not the bird. And the tree?"

I shrugged.

"You don't know much, do you?"

"Less all the time," I admitted ruefully.

She smiled. "That's a good sign. Now, if I were you and this were *my* card," she began....

Playing the Bird in the Tree Card

The bedraggled eagle clings tightly to the high branch of the oak tree, its powerful talons cutting into the deeply serrated grey bark. Or maybe the eagle perches on an ash tree, not an oak—only time will tell. It has flown hard and long, fleeing its death. Unexpectedly, the hunter has become the hunted. The eagle's dark glittering golden eyes dart back and forth, and it turns its head from side to side, raptly alert to danger.

I draw near and it shivers. There is something I recognize in its glance, and I realize it was not always a bird. I sense a kindred spirit, trapped in an unfamiliar form. Too long a changeling, it has forgotten who it truly is.

I know my song can free it, restore its memory and hence its form, if I can find the proper words. I call out: "Turning and turning in the widening gyre—"

The eagle ruffles its feathers but does not transform.

I compose a poem and croon softly in the bird's direction.

"Caught between two worlds,

 a bird that is and isn't

clings to a tree that is and isn't what it appears.

One has forgotten who it was,

the other always knew what it could become.

One is foolish and flies from what it cannot flee;

the other is wise and rooted deeply.

Come to me, the one who seeks to flee

its destiny."

With a whoosh, the eagle flies down from the tree and lands in my lap. I smooth its tattered dark gold feathers, feel its heart pulsating rapidly through its soft, bloodstained breast.

I whisper in its ear—and suddenly it changes into a handsome young man with a spear wound in his chest. I recognize the story and the man.

Long ago, or so it is said, in the land we know as Wales, the virgin Arianrhod ("Silver Wheel") unex-

pectedly gave birth to an infant, later named Lleu Llaw Gyffes, "the Fair-Haired One with the Skillful Hand."

Cursed by his mother never to have a human wife, Lleu and the sorcerers Math and Gwydion find a way to change his solitary circumstance. They create a woman out of flowers. Not just any flowers, but flowers of oak and broom and meadowsweet. They breathe "human" life into her and name her Blodeuwedd, "Flower-Face."

A living, breathing, floral display, she marries Lleu, giving him a wife despite his mother's curse. Blodeuwedd has no choice nor thinks of having any. Created by men to satisfy a man's desire, she is fertile Nature under subjugation, blooming not for herself but only for another.

Happy at first, she slowly realizes her un-natural situation and falls in love with the visiting Lord of Penllyn, Gronw Pebr, a handsome huntsman. Soon the flower-maiden and the lord conspire to murder Lleu. A year after their first embrace, Gronw throws a ritually prepared spear and strikes Lleu, who is straddling a goat while taking a bath next to a stream—but that's quite another story, and the details don't matter here.

Gronw's spear finds its mark but doesn't strike Lleu dead. Lleu transforms into an eagle and flies away. Time passes, a year exactly, and, according to the story, his sorcerer uncle Gwydion tracks him to his perch high in an oak tree. He sings a special song to him to lure him down, and then transforms him back into his human form.

I interrupted the Seer. "Who is Arianrhod? And what happened to Blodeuwedd and her lover? And—

15

even more important—what does this story have to do with me?"

"Be patient. What's your rush? We have plenty of time. In fact, that's all we ever have. Now. This moment. The eternal Present. But since you are so curious, and so impatient, I'll give you a hint. Arianrhod is the ancient Welsh goddess of the moon and stars, linked with the tidal cycles of life and death and rebirth, from which Lleu is fleeing. That is all I will tell you now, since the story must unfold in its own way, in its own time."

She looked at the card. "Where was I? Ah yes. I've called the birdman down from the tree, and he has transformed into himself."

She returned to the story.

T*he handsome youth looks at me in puzzlement.*

"Who are you?" He asks. "You are not my uncle Gwydion."

"Obviously I am not. Nor am I a made-up woman fashioned for your pleasure, like your betraying blossom-bride, Blodeuwedd."

He turns rapacious, his hands opening and closing like powerful talons, his body again taking on the pose of the raptor predator. "She wanted me killed. I, I who gave her life! She would have been nothing but a bouquet of wilting flowers without me."

"You made her only for your desire and never thought of hers. What made you think she would be

'happy ever after' as your fragrant floral plaything, your personal sex slave? No woman alive, not even a flower-maiden, could stay content that way for long, no matter how attractive you think you are."

He looks away, his handsome face set in anger. "She was our creation, my creature to do with as I wished," he proclaims. "Mine by right, to claim my right to rule."

"No wonder she sought love with someone else and wanted you to die, tired of such subjugation. Besides, by what right did you create life?"

"It's all my mother's fault. She cursed me at my birth, depriving me of what was justly mine—the Sovereignty of the Land which I could only claim through marriage."

"I see you still take no responsibility. My sympathies lie with Flower-Face."

He raises his hand to strike me.

I raise my hand in warning. "Remember—it is I who enabled you to change back into human form. In your flighty year, your year of flight, you had forgotten who you truly are: a human being. Though perhaps your raptor-shape is more in keeping with your actual nature." I pause a moment, pondering. "Perhaps you have never known who you truly are."

He frowns in puzzlement. "What do you mean, 'who you truly are'?"

"What kind of man thinks only of his own gratification and uses another being as a kind of animated toy? Fragrant, sweet, in full blossom—your selfish domina-

17

tion is a most unnatural relationship to have with a woman. Or with Nature. In this case, they are both so obviously the same."

He has enough self-awareness to begin to feel ashamed. He scrapes his foot along the ground, not looking up.

"I wanted to marry, but my mother, Arianrhod, refused to let that happen."

"She has her part in this, but so do you."

"I loved the flower-maiden. She was sweet, so simple—so uncomplicated. And mine, all mine, with never a thought for anyone else—until that noble huntsman arrived while I was gone." He suddenly shifts his mood again. "She betrayed me, and tricked me, and wanted me dead. A fate I barely managed to avoid."

"And only for a while," I point out. "Death comes to us all, including you, and takes us somewhere else. Your mother knows all about that, with her silver-wheeled chariot and her oar-wheeled boat."

Dusk is settling in the air, speckling daylight with a sprinkle of dusty confetti. The full moon rises. A thorn tree bursts into bloom, its soft white blossoms contrasting sharply with its red berries and dagger-sharp spikes.

Lleu looks at the thorn tree and then the oak tree and his eyes widen in surprise. The oak has morphed, as had he, from one kind of living being to another. Now it is a mighty ash, with rigid grey bark and enormous limbs. A serpent gnaws at its roots. It is the World Tree,

Yggdrasil, stretching from Earth to Heaven, transecting the Three Worlds.

A beautiful owl with a flower-like face perches delicately on a low branch, its brown and white feathers forming a cowl around its heart-shaped head.

"Hoot … hoot … hoot …." The owl proclaims. Lleu looks at it in shock.

I sense another kindred soul lost in a transformed shape. I struggle to find the proper words to sing it back to itself.

I address it solemnly: "You who see what is hidden in darkness, herald of death, bringer of wisdom. You who see what others cannot, observing in silence, bearer of truth through dreams. You who see into the hidden places of the soul and hear the faint sounds of distant thoughts … now is the time, the time has come now, to transform back into your true self, into who you truly are. Let it be so!"

The owl peers at me, blinking, moving its head rapidly from side to side, shifting uneasily from one taloned foot to the other upon the branch. I realize my incantation has only encouraged it to stay in its present form. I am sure, however, I know who it really is. I find a better set of words.

"You who are the fertility of the Earth bursting forth into fragrant blossom—you who were shaped by hu-

19

man hands into a semblance of humanity, return now to your flower-maiden form. Leave behind your wings of flight and root yourself back into the earth once more. Whatever your true nature, flower or human, you are a creature of the land, not of the skies. Remember who you are and return to what you might become. Let it be so!"

Silently, the owl flaps its wings, glides down from its branch, and settles in my lap. I caress its soft, mottled feathers and whisper a name in its ear. It trembles and transforms into a beautiful young woman wearing a multi-colored mantle of woven grasses and fragrant flowers. Her breath smells like lavender, her delicate pink skin resembles rose petals.

She looks around in confusion. Seeing the young man with dried blood on his chest, she starts to shake—not with fear but with rage.

"You!" She cries out in a voice as thorny as a rose. "You used me for your own desires! You never gave a thought about my needs, my satisfaction! You denied me my own nature. First your sorcerer friends turned me into a human, and then into an owl, mobbed by other birds, living alone in darkness."

He steps forward, fist raised. "Ungrateful creature! I gave you life and you betrayed me. You owe everything to me, but you used your sexual wiles to conspire to have me killed. You deserve your fate!"

"And you yours!"

Accusations thicken the air. The flower-maiden's mantle starts to wilt and shed its blossoms on the *ground; the man begins to turn back into an eagle, fingers morphing into cruelly curving talons, tearing at the ground.*

I hold up my hands. "Stop! Stop and listen!" I command. "Yours is the epic struggle of all who forget their true nature and who deny the natural cycle of life and death."

Shocked into silence, they stare at me in puzzlement.

"You, Lleu—you have used Nature for your own purposes and satisfaction, without consideration of others, driven by your desire to dominate. You have turned Nature's selflessly offered bounty of plants and flowers into an unnatural form: the semblance of a woman. No wonder she dissembled."

The flower-maiden preens herself, pleased with my declaration.

I turn to her. "And you, Blodeuwedd, were unfaithful and wished your husband dead. You have confused sex and fecundity with love, and stopped at nothing in your quest for freedom."

Lleu smiles at that.

I take another, deeper breath and continue. "There is enough blame to pass around and no profit in the passing. Ask instead: how can humans and Nature live in peace, with mutual respect and mutual appreciation? How can each of you discover your true selves, based on deeper sympathy?

"Both of you, remember this: even the most fragrant flowers in bloom carry within themselves the harbin-

gers of death, for they will soon fade and wilt. Nothing lasts forever. Only Love endures, but neither of you know anything about that—Lleu, because you choose not to; Blodeuwedd, because it is not in your flower-like nature."

The sky has darkened now, and I can barely see their faces. I hear a strange rasping sound, like the spinning of a metal disk grating against metal. A horse-drawn chariot with silver wheels comes whirling out of the full moon and lands beside us.

A tall, radiant woman dressed in white descends. Her face is moon-shaped, glowing with reflected light; her hair glitters like spun silver. "I am the Silver Disc that descends into the Sea," she declares. She gestures to the eagle-man and flower-maiden. "I have come for both of you, that you may continue your journey of self-discovery in the next world, the world that awaits you after life." Like somnambulists, they climb into her chariot.

Arianrhod looks at me and smiles, a smile that gleams like moonlight dancing over water. "You have passed the second test," she says. Her voice sounds like stardust.

She flicks the reins and the horse gallops into the sky, heading toward the Corona Borealis or perhaps the Milky Way—or perhaps the chariot turns into a silver-wheeled ship and sinks into the sea. It's hard to tell, even with the full moon lending its mirrored light.

Thoughtfully, the Seer turned the card face-down and stirred it into the swirling pile upon the mirror-top table.

I shuddered suddenly.

"Someone walk over your grave?" She asked.

"What did you say?"

"Just an expression we use where I come from."

"It's just—all this stuff about death…. The first card had the ferryman, the raven, and the shrouded figure on the other side of the river. This one has the owl, the moon goddess, and her chariot. Or maybe it's a boat."

"Ah, yes. The psychopomps. The ones who lead the souls to the Other Side. You're right. There have been several." She hesitated and tilted her head for a moment, as if listening to something. "I rarely give advice, but this time I will. It's never too soon—or too late—to make friends with Death."

"Make friends with Death?"

"That's what I said. Don't repeat. You sound like a parrot."

I ignored her sharp reply. "You're saying there's a message in the cards about Death drawing near?" I looked at her with a worried frown. Was I attracting Death, or perhaps was Death attracting me? I shivered again. "And what did the moon goddess mean when she said, 'You have passed the second test.' What was the test? And who passed it? Me or you?" I took a deep breath. "And even more important, what does it mean for me?"

"Excellent questions, searching for good answers. But then, what is a 'good' answer? 'Yes'? 'No'? Or, 'It all depends'? Remember what I said when we began: There is no future, only possibilities. Besides, it all depends on the question. And often the question we ask is not the question we need to ask, not the deep, true question that is eagerly seeking to be answered."

She pointed at the reflections on the table. "Draw another card."

I took a deep breath and stretched out my hand.

✳

The Scribe interrupted me. "Wait a moment! I need to sharpen my pen." He flexed his fingers and stretched his arms. "You talk really fast. There's a lot to write down in such a short time."

"I suppose I am talking quickly. That's because my story is long and the night is short." I shifted my position on the blanket. The sand dune was a hard cushion to lean against, especially at my age. I watched as he whittled at the point of his pen.

Hesitantly, he said, "I know I'm just a scribe, but I have some questions, if you don't mind. I want to make sure the transcript is clear and complete."

I nodded.

"So ... all this happened long ago, before you became a teacher, right?"

I nodded again. "Yes, long before I became a teacher. I was young and lost, uncertain of my way. I was a no-nothing who didn't know how little I knew. The only thing I knew was that I was lost in every possible way."

"And you were wandering around this old town and saw a sign on a used book store. Were there many bookstores in the area?"

"No, nor any other shops that I recall."

"How unlikely is that!"

"Indeed."

"Not that I doubt your story—your reputation as a truth-teller is impeccable. I'm just curious, you see. And the bookstore? Can you tell me more about it?"

I smiled. "It was unusual, to say the least. Full of cobwebs and endless corridors. A wrought-iron circular staircase led up to another level—but I didn't know that then. It took a long time to discover it."

The scribe nodded. "Thanks. I guess that gives me a clearer picture. Let's get back to the story. I don't want you to lose the thread."

"Yes, at my age, that's an easy thing to do, even if Ariadne is close by."

"Ariadne?"

"The Spider goddess. But more about her later."

The Scribe opened his notebook again and prepared to write.

✳

I stirred the cards, creating a maelstrom of pictures shifting beneath my hands. One rose up. I turned it over. A burning bush, a bird.

The Seer began, "If I were you, and this were *my* card…."

Playing the Burning Bush Card

I have walked a great distance, forded many rivers, and climbed many mountains. I have struggled across endless deserts and through dense, deep forests. I have found my way and been lost again and found it and lost it again and again, so many times I have lost count.

I do not know how long I have wandered, nor for what I seek. I hope I will know it when I find it, though I live in fear that perhaps what I seek has come and gone and I have failed to notice. Perhaps all there is, is wandering.

I walk alone. All my companions have long departed, for they are traveling other paths in this world or the next.

My pack that once was heavy is now light, for I have gradually left behind most of what I carried. I am surprised by how little I need and how much of what I carry weighs me down.

I have water and food, but not too much of either, trusting that my needs will be met and that, if not, I will need less than I might suppose. A gourd, decorated with a scallop shell, dangles from my staff.

Suddenly I reach a crossroads. I know not which way to go. Perhaps the path I choose to travel does not matter, but perhaps it does. I sit in the middle of the crossroads and wait for a sign, an indication. I wait and wait, and eventually the sun sets. The new moon may have risen but I cannot tell because it is the new moon and because clouds eclipse the stars. I sit and wait. I wait and sit.

There is nowhere to go, nothing to do.

The night grows cold, the darkness more profound. I listen to the sounds of stars turning on their axes, of the Earth beneath me shifting and creaking, expanding and contracting. Birds twitter, bid each other good night, and then are still. A large cat yowls in the distance, or perhaps it yawns. I cannot tell and cannot seek the answer.

And then, suddenly, in the depth of the unrelenting darkness of the night, I see a distant glimmer. A faint light begins to glow, and I hear the crackling of flames. I smell the slightly acrid scent of something burning.

Perhaps this is the sign I have been waiting for.

Stiff from sitting on the cold, damp ground, I struggle to my feet. I pick up my pack and staff, and slowly I begin walking toward the light.

I approach and see a burning bush. Perched on top is a brilliantly colored bird, its torso purple-red, its legs pink, its talons gold. Or maybe there is no bush but only the bird, burning. Now I see—the bush is burning

and so is the bird, lighting up the night and fluttering its smoldering wings to fan the flames. I watch in horror as the bird mutely emolliates itself. Only the flames crackle and pop. The bird is silent, emitting neither cries of pain nor throaty sounds of exultation.

In what seems like no time at all—and perhaps it isn't—all that is left is a pile of smoking grey ash. All color is gone, all light, and all the flame-fed warmth.

I notice now that a different light begins to dispel the darkness: dawn has come. The sun is rising, and the pile of ashes shifts in the early morning breeze. It stirs and trembles and gradually takes form. A small bird with brilliant plumage rises from the ashes, preens its dusty feathers, and stretches its newly formed gossamer wings. While I watch, the Phoenix grows to maturity and then, with a flap of its now-powerful wings, it rises to meet the sun.

I didn't know what to say, so I said nothing.

The Seer waited patiently.

At last I observed, "More death. But this time, there is also resurrection."

She nodded and waited.

"I understand part of the lesson here. We carry much more than we need. We carry all kinds of baggage, old habits, old wounds, old resentments. Stuff that holds us back."

She smiled with approval.

Encouraged, I continued. "I wonder what all this wandering means. This person is looking for something and doesn't know what it is but continues wandering. Maybe they have forgotten what they are looking for—or maybe they never knew. But they keep wandering."

The Seer replied, "One of my favorite authors wrote, 'Not all who wander are lost.' But perhaps this person is." She tilted her head to one side and stared at me. "This card has special meaning for you, I see."

"You're right, it does. I've been a pilgrim on the Camino de Santiago, carrying a staff with a scallop shell, just like that seeker. I, too, was searching for something."

"Did you find it?"

I shook my head. "Maybe, or maybe not. I do not know. Maybe I did but I forgot, or maybe I didn't recognize it when I found it."

"Finding what you seek depends on asking the right question, the deepest question. That's why it's called a quest. And then, of course, you need to recognize the answer when it comes. That's called discernment. And then—and then, you need to act upon it."

She dropped the card back on the pile. "I think we've done enough. Besides, I have another obligation."

Startled at this sudden termination of our session, I asked, "Can I come back?"

"That is for me to know and you to wonder. Just remember: Nothing—not time, not you, not me—is what it seems."

With that, she looked down at the table and began stirring the cards. "Until next time, if there is one. Same time—" she laughed that odd, barking laugh, "Same place. Perhaps."

Abruptly dismissed, I stood up, my chair scraping on the floor. I walked out the door and closed it behind me. The bookstore was empty. I let myself out and heard the doorbell tinkling behind me.

Two

A week later I returned. I entered the bookstore and knocked on the closet door. A voice called out, "Come in."

Everything looked just the same. In fact, nothing had changed, not even the Seer's clothes. She was still sitting at the mirror-top table, which was still covered with its mirage of cards; her purse still dangled from the back of the Plexiglas chair.

"I'm glad you are still here," I said, with an unexpected sense of relief.

She welcomed me with a wry smile. "It was time for you to return."

"I feel like I never left. Or rather, I feel like I was only gone for a moment."

"There is no time but now," she reminded me. "And now is the time to continue."

She pointed to the empty chair, but I stood by the door, not yet ready to enter further.

"I have a lot of questions to ask you, and this time I would really like some answers."

She raised her hand imperiously. "Now is not the time." She touched a long, red-tipped finger to her lips, indicating I was to be silent.

Stubbornly, I continued, "There's one question you shouldn't mind answering. What do you charge?"

She looked at me, her finger still pressed against her lips.

I continued, "The first reading was free, according to the advertisement. But what about the second? How much do you charge?"

She smiled. "There are different charges, depending on the readings. In your case, I haven't yet decided what I'll ask you to pay."

"But—"

"Enough. Now is not the time, even if the time is always Now. Choose your card, or let the card choose you."

Again, I found my resistance dissolving. Her will was like a force of nature that I could not defy—nor was I sure I wanted to. After all, I still felt lost, and she seemed to have the answers. Or at least, a way to access answers. At least I hoped she did. Besides, I was curious about what would happen next. So I did as I was told.

I sat down in my chair and stirred the cards again. A card stuck to my palm. This time, I looked at it before handing it to the Seer. I saw a stone well with its wooden cover pulled off to one side. I gave her the card.

She smiled. "If I were you, and this were *my* card," She began….

Playing the Well with the Staircase Card

I have come to this holy well seeking wisdom or healing or maybe just … seeking. I don't know and it doesn't matter. What I think I seek may not be what I seek after all, and certainly may not be what I find.

The ancient well is in the middle of a bright green meadow dotted with blood-red poppies and surrounded by dense woodland. There is no visible path leading to the well, so I cut across the boggy ground, leaving a trail of bent grasses behind me like a wake.

The scarred wooden well-cover lies propped on the ground, leaning against the moss-covered stone casing that surrounds the well. I peer inside, expecting to find a winch, a bucket, and a ladle. Instead I see a spiraling stone staircase leading down into darkness.

I look around. There is no one within sight. A faint crescent moon, shaped like a slender "C," shines dimly in the sky, and a breeze rustles the leaves in the surrounding trees. Branches rub and creak against each other, and ripples of ruffled grass spread across the meadow in rhythmic waves. I smell fresh-turned earth, rotting vegetation, and the faint scent of honey.

Curiosity killed the cat they say, but I am determined to find out what lies within, so I lean my backpack and hiking stick against the well. Then I orient to the seven directions and recite a prayer of protection: "May the doors and gates and paths between the worlds be open to me, and may the doors and gates and paths of all those who wish to do me or those I love any harm, be closed. May it be so!"

I swing up and over the waist-high stone casing and down onto the first step. The slippery stones are worn unevenly from millennia of use. I begin my descent, spiraling ever deeper, my right hand brushing lightly against the damp stone wall to steady myself. A carved

labyrinth marks my passage, and I stop to trace its seven-fold path with my fingers. Slowly, the light of day becomes dim and faint, receding to a distant circle, like the sun at midnight. My right hand finds and traces another carving in the wall: a triple spiral.

Gradually my eyes adjust to the deepening darkness. I hear the faint plop-plop-plop of dripping water. I must be approaching the spring. The staircase ends abruptly, and I carefully step off into near-obscurity. I follow the sound to its source, springing from the Earth herself.

The bubbling spring wells out of the ground and splatters onto the nearby rocks. The air smells of damp earth after a rain. I am suddenly very thirsty. The water seems to glow faintly, and I see a glistening salmon swimming back and forth, lazily flicking its shining tail. And I notice a metal chalice and a cauldron left nearby on the hard-packed floor. I reach for the cup to dip it in the water, when a sonorous voice calls out.

"Have you asked permission?"

Startled, I pause, cup almost in hand, and peer into the darkness. I hear no sound of breathing, of rustling clothing. Perhaps I imagined the voice. I reach toward the cup again.

Again the voice rings out, louder and more insistent this time. "I say again: Have you asked permission?"

I call out with false bravado, "Who wants to know?"

I hear a deep chuckle, and a tall, hooded figure draws near, leaning on a staff. He uncovers a lantern, which casts a faint golden glow around him. A small pig walks beside him, and a wren perches on his right shoulder. The man (if humankind he is, I can't be sure) has a face that resembles an ancient oak tree, deeply furrowed and mottled grey with age. Bright obsidian eyes peer out from under white, bushy eyebrows.

"I have been waiting for you to come."

"Me?"

"You, or someone like you. It doesn't matter who. So I ask again, this is the third time—three times's the charm—Have you asked permission?"

This time I have a better answer ready. "I ask permission now, though I do not know of whom to ask it. Perhaps of the salmon that wisely swims idly back and forth, or perhaps of the Spirit who guards these sacred waters. Or perhaps of you."

Another chuckle. "You learn fast. You have potential, or at least you have possibility."

I wait, uneasy and thirsty.

He makes an expansive gesture. "Now you can drink your fill."

I pick up the ornate metal chalice. In the gloom, I can't make out the pattern on its side, but I can feel its complexity beneath my fingers. I dip it in the spring until it overflows. The water has the fragrance of orange blossoms and the flavor of ambrosia. I swirl it in my mouth, savoring the taste and slippery, satin-smooth texture.

I fill the cup again and offer it to the sorcerer, for such I presume him to be.

He thanks me and drains the chalice, wipes it dry with his sleeve, then replaces it beside the cauldron.

"Did you see the Salmon of Knowledge and make a wish?" He asks.

"A wish?"

"Those who see the salmon in the sacred spring will have their wish fulfilled."

"Good news!" I exclaim. "I saw the salmon and now I will make a wish."

He looks at me with a foxy grin. "You must recite the wish while looking at the salmon. No fish, no wish fulfilment. Look again."

I stare into the reflecting waters, but the salmon is gone.

"Perhaps next time," he says dismissively.

Pointing with the sharpened end of his staff, he directs me toward a barely visible door in the far wall of the circular chamber.

Surprised, I ask, "You mean there's more to see? Not just the spring?"

He smiles wryly. "Your journey has just begun."

Stumbling in the semi-darkness, I reach the massive wooden door. It appears to be decorated with two twining snakes, or maybe they are two twining dragons. They seem to be moving in a slow, sinuous dance. I look again and they are still. Perhaps it was a trick of light—or darkness.

The heavy wrought-iron handle does not turn. I push against the door with my shoulder; it doesn't budge.

The door is locked. There is no doorbell. I turn back to ask advice, but there is no one in the room, at least no one I can see.

Surely there must be a way to open the door, I tell myself. If not, why did the mage direct me to it? I start recalling magical door-opening phrases. "Open Sesame," I intone. No good. "Abracadabra!" I shout. "Please," I petition humbly. Nada.

I press my fingers into the stones on either side of the doorframe, looking for a hidden switch, a sudden-sinking piece of masonry. Nothing shifts. Then I remember what the sorcerer said. Perhaps it was a hint.

I knock three times, the sound dying abruptly after each strike.

A previously unseen shutter creaks opens in the door, and a gruff voice demands, "What time is it?"

I look at my wristwatch, but I realize it stopped running long ago, though how long ago I have no way of knowing. I know what time it was but not what time it is. I wonder if I should make a guess, but then remember what I have learned.

I solemnly declare, "There is no time but now."

The speaker clears his throat but doesn't open the door. Not a complete rejection, I realize, but I haven't got the answer right, at least not quite.

I try again. "The time is always now."

He sighs, perhaps with relief, as do I.

"You may come in."

The door swings open, and I step onto a narrow ledge in a very small shaft with a metal ladder extending downwards. There is no one here but me and nothing here except bare stone walls and a very deep hole with a rusty ladder. Above me is a dark ceiling speckled with twinkling stars.

There is nowhere to go but down—unless I want to go back, and I doubt I can retrace my steps, nor do I want to. I want to know—I need to know—where this journey will lead and maybe where it will end. The door slams closed behind me.

Cautiously, I start climbing down the ladder, which seems to extend down into the center of the Earth. My boots clang dully against the worn, flaking metal rungs. I keep descending, pausing periodically to wipe away the sweat that is trickling down my face. The air is dusty and stale.

My legs begin to tremble from the strain, my arms quiver. There is something hypnotic about my repetitive movement, the sound of my steps reverberating against the walls of the shaft. I struggle to keep my focus sharp. I do not want to fall.

At last I see a glimmer of light below that grows brighter as I descend. By the time I reach the bottom, the light is so bright that I am temporarily blinded. Disoriented, I slip off the ladder. Fortunately, my feet touch ground. When I can see again, I realize I am in a large cavern. Rainbow-colored light reflects off the uneven, crystal-covered walls. It's like being inside an immense, glittering geode.

I look around in awe at the sparkling chamber. I notice a group of tall, ethereal women at one end of the room. I approach them slowly.

One has a drop spindle in her hand and spins fine thread while I watch, mesmerizing me with the whirling movement. Another sits at a loom, weaving a complex pattern of many colors. I watch her weave one row and then another, throwing a carved bone shuttle back and forth through alternating layers of thread. Another seems to be spinning moonbeams.

They watch me curiously.

"A goddess's dress is seamless," I observe.

They nod in approval and whisper to each other.

Three weary old women limp forward from the shadows and challenge me. "Who do you think we are?" they ask, their voices a discordant blur.

I struggle to put my best words forward. "You are the Spinners of our human fate, the weavers of the patterns of our lives. You measure the thread of our days and sometimes cut it short, or so it seems to us."

When Truth speaks through you, you know it by the goose-bumps on your flesh. Feeling the hairs rise on my arms, I continue: "You sit at the hub of the starry Wheel and your distaff and spindle turn the Earth and planets in the sky. One of your relations helped Theseus find his way through the maze by unravelling a ball of yarn, and yet you can also make our lives come unraveled."

40

They seem to like what I am saying, so I keep speaking. "Without you, there would be no stories woven out of words, no raveling and unravelling tales, no threads of lifetimes to pursue, no twining spirit cords. And, sometimes, you even spin flax into gold."

They look me over carefully, whispering among themselves. I wait, uncomfortable. I know the Fates themselves are judging me.

They speak together, their words overlapping, slightly out of synch. "Why are you here?"

"I do not know, but perhaps it is my Fate." *They smile at that.*

Encouraged, I continue, "I was looking for a holy well, and I descended a spiral staircase and asked permission to drink the water in the spring and answered a question and opened a door and descended a ladder … and here I am. Truly, I am only passing through—or will be, if there is somewhere else for me to go and if the Fates will let me leave."

They reply in discordant harmony, "Of course you are only passing through. That is the nature of human existence, to always and only be passing through."

The weaver goddesses leave their work and come forward. Perhaps they are curious to see a human being up close. I doubt they have many visitors here in their chamber within the Land.

A dark, hunched-over, spider-like woman joins the group.

41

The Fates whisper to her, and she nods in agreement, then draws near, trailing a luminous thread. "Your presence here has been most diverting. It is good to know our importance has not been forgotten in the Upper World—which you know as the Middle Realm. We will give you a ball of thread to carry with you. Perhaps, like Theseus, you will be able to wind it up and find your way home—if that be your fate."

The spider-woman hands me a tiny ball of thread, light as a puff of cottonwood seeds. The ball is already mostly unwound, and the thread leads across the floor. Unlike Theseus, who unraveled a ball of thread to mark his return passage, I would be doing the reverse: someone had already unwound the thread to mark my way.

I take the cloud-like wisp of thread gratefully. "I thank all of you for your help. And may the thread of my life be long and strong!"

They smile but give me no assurances.

I follow the unraveled thread, winding it up as I go, wondering where I will find its end—or its beginning.

The thread disappears down a hole in the floor. This time there is no ladder to clamber down, but there is a thick, multi-strand cord dangling into darkness. I swing into the hole, grab the twisting, twining rope, and carefully lower myself down, and down, and further down. The glittering world of the fateful weaver goddesses fades into a point of light surrounded by a void. The ground below rises to meet me, and I drop the cord but hold fast to the ball of gossamer thread. I rewind the thread and catch my breath.

There is no light in this dark space, yet I sense that I am inside a living cavern, a womb carved within Mother Earth. Sunlight has never penetrated this deep. The air, which I cannot see, caresses my skin like black velvet. In the Weavers' glittering chamber I was blinded by light; here I am blinded by obscurity.

In this unrelenting darkness, suddenly the ball of thread begins to glow, and I slowly make out the outline of a twice-life-size stone statue that fills the center of the cavern. I recognize her. She is the Earth Mother in her Isis guise, life-giving and compassionate, seated on her throne. Her falcon-headed child, Horus, here shape-shifted into a stone bird, perches on her lap. His left eye is damaged from his battle with his uncle Seth.

I follow the luminous thread. Its end is held in Horus's stony beak.

My feet make no sound as I walk up to the statue and clamber up its legs onto its knees. Suddenly the stone falcon blinks. His left eye glows like the moon, his right like the sun. He flaps his wings; he grows; he grabs me in his talons and swoops me up through layers of fading darkness, up to the realm of soil and grass and sun. Together we soar over tree and water, hill and valley, seeing far, seeing long. I see—too much to tell and much that cannot be told.

Gently, the falcon Horus drops me onto the soft, bent grass beside the well in the middle of the meadow. Lying on my back, I watch him fly away, becoming a tiny dark dot surrounded by blue. He disappears. The crescent moon hangs faintly in the bright sky. It doesn't appear to have moved.

I breathe in the fresh green scent of meadow grass and flowers. I bask in the breeze brushing through my hair, and I run my fingers through the soil, uncovering a beetle pushing a ball of dirt. A butterfly flutters down to rest upon a crinkled poppy petal beside my nose. The moon begins to move again across the sky.

Slowly, somewhat shakily, I stand up. Hands raised, I declare, "May the doors and gates and paths between the worlds be closed! May it be so."

I lift up my backpack, pick up my hiking stick, and, following the wake I made in the meadow, I walk back towards the rustling woods.

The Seer replaced the card face-down on the mirror top. As she turned it over, I noticed that the previously colorful design had faded into a sepia shadow of itself.

I sat in silence, puzzling over the story. At last I asked, "I thought you said the future is only possibility. But you—or I—just met the Fates, who say they spin our lives and cut them short if that is their desire. Isn't that a contradiction?"

She smiled. "There are three Fates, not one, and they are not always in agreement. They'd like you to believe they are all-powerful, but what makes you think your destiny is set? Weavers can unravel as well as weave. There's room for movement and manipulation. Odysseus's wife, Penelope, wove her elderly father-in-law's shroud each day and secretly unraveled it every night to delay her suitors."

"I'm not convinced."

"You think that matters?" She scoffed. "It's a story that not only has 'something' to do with you, it's also a story that has something to do *with* you. To quote a master storyteller again, 'A story is our shortest route to the meaning of things, and our easiest way to remember and carry the meaning we discover.'"

I thought back over the readings. "There's the recurring theme of Death."

"Inevitable."

"It makes me uncomfortable."

"Of course. You are being confronted with a truth that you have tried to avoid."

"You mean, these card readings aren't just for entertainment?" I replied defensively—and immediately regretted it.

She gave me a disgusted look. "Do you really think you were called here to be entertained? If so, you are a bigger fool than I imagined. Reading these cards is deadly serious. Remember, you came here with a question."

"You're right. I am a fool. A skeptic and a fool." With difficulty, I continued, "You have to realize, this kind of thing—these 'readings'—are completely foreign to me. I'm a skeptic, a dis-believer by nature. Truth is, I wouldn't be here if I didn't feel so desperate."

"I know why you are here. Do you?" She looked at me and sighed. "There are patterns that reveal—the cards, for example—and patterns that conceal. You are mired in the latter. The cards give you the chance, albeit a small chance, to change your habits. If this were my card, I would say that confronting Death is a way for you to truly begin to live."

I stared at the swirling cards and changed the subject. "Did I—or you—pass another test?"

"What do you think?"

"I think there were several: at the spring, at the locked door, getting past the Fates, and the Earth Mother."

"It's possible."

I mused, "I wonder how many tests there are and what happens at the end."

"Don't we all," she sighed. Then she pointed at the table. "Time to draw another card."

"Not yet," I said firmly. "I have another question. Who is passing all these tests? Me or you?"

"Remember, I start each reading saying, 'If I were you and this were my card….'"

"What's that supposed to mean? I draw the cards, so the reading should be about me, but you are in the story you tell, not me."

"Is that what you think?" She seemed annoyed, or maybe she was just amused. "I am a Seer. I am trained to be your impartial substitute, your 'stand-in.' It's a discipline learnt with much effort over many years. However, if you're not satisfied with my reading of the cards, perhaps you need to learn to read your own cards." Her eyes flashed. "That is, if you dare."

Much to my surprise, I heard myself asking, "Will you teach me how?"

"To read the cards?" She frowned. "I rarely take on students. In fact, it's been ages. Literally, ages."

"Believe me, I rarely take on a teacher. In fact, it never crossed my mind to ask until this moment. You brought the topic up, and the goose-bumps on my arms told me that you are right. I need to learn to read my own story in the cards."

"Can you pay the price? And are you willing to?" She pointed to the pile once again. "Now, draw your card."

I reached forward and stirred the cards. I drew the card that drew me to it: a child sitting forlornly by the sea. I handed it to her.

She took the card and nodded. "If I were you, and this were *my* card…."

✳

The Scribe interrupted my recital. "Wait! Stop! Sorry, but I need a break."

He stood up and wandered off behind a dune. He soon returned with an embarrassed smile. "Ah, that feels much better. Too much tea, too late at night."

I waited while he settled back against the dune.

Hesitantly, he said, "Were you really a skeptic, a disbeliever?"

I nodded.

"I mean—I know you never lie, but it's so hard to imagine the 'you' you were, becoming the 'you' you are."

"That's why I want to tell my story now, before it is too late." I opened the thermos and took a sip of hot chai, enjoying the scents of cinnamon and cardamom, the whiff of vanilla that tickled my nose. "This is quite good."

The Scribe smiled. "Thanks! It's an old family recipe." He paged through his notebook. "You mention having goose-bumps on your arms. Is that an important sign for knowing Truth?"

"There are many signs, and we each have to find the sign that works for us. For some people, it's a shivery feeling in their belly. For others, it's goose-bumps or *piel de gallina*—that's Spanish for 'chicken-skin.' We each have our own ways of knowing. Just as the Seer wasn't willing to interpret the meaning of the cards for me, I can't tell you what your 'way of knowing' is. You have to become still, go within, and listen to your own inner wisdom."

The Scribe stopped writing and became very still. After a few minutes, he replied, "Now that I think about it, I realize that sometimes my nose twitches."

I nodded.

"Not because I'm afraid of something. More like, I'm in the 'presence' of something extra-real."

The Scribe began writing frantically. He finished and looked up. "Thanks! That's really worthwhile information."

"Worth staying up all night and recording my story?"

He nodded seriously. "Worth a lot more than that."

✳

Playing the Child by the Sea card

The dark-haired child sits forlornly looking out to sea. The coarse sand beach is riddled with shards of shells and browning clumps of bulbous kelp. Here, a rounded piece of sea-polished glass; there, a tide-tossed pebble. The air is laden with the iodine smell of the sea. Waves suck in and out at the shore, leaving saliva-like foam and ripples in their wake.

A call breaks the air, a harsh, keening bark. The child turns toward the sound and sees, in the distance, a sleek dark shape hauling itself onto a pile of sea-surrounded boulders. The child leaps up and runs, splashing bare-foot through tide and time, which wait for no one.

A watery gulf separates the child from its rocky goal, but the child makes a leap of faith and desperation, hurling across the no-man's zone between shore and sea and catapulting up against the cold wet chest of the waiting seal. Its whiskers tickle the child as it nuzzles against its slick, furry breast.

"I knew you'd come back," the child whispers.

The seal watches, blinking, its fingered flippers flapping rhythmically against the dripping, sea-splashed rocks. It cries again, a gentler bark, and then another. Its body forms a shelter for the child, who leans against its chest and listens to its slow-beating heart. The child falls asleep, lulled by the seal's rhythmic breathing. Rather than reeking of fetid rotting fish, this seal smells of iodine and seaweed.

The tide rises slowly but as inevitably as the moon, and before long the pile of boulders, the seal, and the child are marooned far from shore. The foaming water rises and falls with the inhale and exhale of the ocean, and the child begins to float up and down against the animal's side. The short flippers of the seal cannot grasp the child, cannot hold it close. It looks at the child with watery dark eyes and rubs its cold damp nose against the child's face, nudging it awake.

Instantly alert, the child understands and climbs up on the broad, slippery back. The child lies prone and

embraces the seal's thick and sinuous neck. With ut-
most care, the seal slips into the sea and swims toward
shore, exquisitely careful of its precious burden.

The Seer looked up but seemed not to see. She paused her recitation, suddenly mute.

After a few minutes, though perhaps it was only a moment in this only-present Now, I broke the spell. Or at any rate, I broke the silence. "That's all you see? A child on a seal heading back to shore? What happens next?"

She shook her head. "I do not know. It is a story that resonates with others I have known, but it shifts in the telling."

"There must be more to the story."

Impatiently, she replied, "Of course there is! But at this moment I can't tell you how the story will unfold nor if I should reveal its ending."

She hesitated and cocked her head as if listening to a sound outside of human range. She stared at me with her unblinking gaze. "Are you sure you want me to continue?"

I nodded with more assurance than I felt. "I'm sure."

She sighed. "Sometimes these stories, like life, don't end well. Or rather, don't end the way we want. But end they must. And follow this story to the end we must. So we will re-enter the card and see what more is waiting to be revealed."

She continued the reading.

They draw close to land, the seal and its treasured cargo. A shout startles them both, and then the loud "crack" of a gunshot. People are standing on the shore.

The seal pauses, hesitant to continue swimming toward almost-certain death. It feels the weight of the child on its back, hugging it around its neck. It shudders and continues toward the group of humans standing on the beach.

A man raises his gun again. Another shot and then another. This time, the bullet finds its target, and blood spurts from the seal's breast. With an inhuman effort (it is a seal, after all), it leaps forward to the shore. The child slips off its back and tumbles onto the coarse, hard-packed sand.

The hunter and his companions run to the fallen forms, shouting at each other with surprise. One grabs the child to keep it out of harm, though what harm could now befall is anybody's guess. The hunter kicks the seal with his rough-shod foot. The seal moves spasmodically and then lies still, its life-blood flowing out in rust-red rivulets to the sea.

Slowly, the seal begins a peculiar transformation, shedding its furry skin like an outsized overcoat. It groans and moans, stretches and twists, releasing itself from a shape it can no longer hold.

Shorn of her pelt, a beautiful, dark-eyed woman lies bleeding to death on the sand. The child wriggles free from the man who holds it and rushes forward, brushing loving hands through the woman's matted dark-brown hair, wiping sand out of her now slack mouth.

The child embraces the woman and cries, and its tears mingle with the Selkie's all-too-human blood.

The child turns to the hunter in rage. "She saved me from drowning in the sea—and you, you killed her!"

The hunter begins to make excuses. "I thought she was a seal with fur I could sell and meat I could eat. I swear I didn't know she was a Selkie. I didn't see you riding on her back."

Suddenly, the hunter starts to weep, convulsing with long-held grief. The humans watch silently. They wait now for him to explain himself.

At last he speaks to the child, wiping his tears with a bloody hand. A red smear marks his cheeks. "She left me shortly after you were born. I told you that your mother left, but I never told you what she was or where she went. She was a Selkie. I fell in love with her when I saw her combing her hair on the beach, and I hid her sealskin pelt in a locked chest out of sight, hoping to hold her in her human form. But one day she discovered the skin and put it on. When I returned, I found you playing in the sand. Her footprints led into the water but did not return. She was gone."

The child looks at the father with contempt. "Each seal you killed—and you've killed many—could have been her. You wished her dead with every shot you fired."

The man looks at the child in puzzlement and wonder. "How did you find her? How did you know she was your mother?"

Without a word, the child turns away and walks into the sea. As if to the water born, the child dives and bobs and swims out toward the setting sun. Gradually its two legs unite as one and its dark brown hair turns sleek and glistens like seal fur in the fading light.

The card fell face-down from the Seer's limp hand. We sat in silence.

At last I observed, "More death. More death and more shape-shifting."

She shifted on the Plexiglas chair.

I added, "This time, no psychopomps."

"That could be a good thing, or bad. It is usually helpful to have a guide."

More silence.

"Perhaps you've had enough?" She asked.

I shook my head. "I still don't know the answer to my question."

"What makes you think there is one? More importantly, are you sure you know the question, the *real* question, the most important one?" Her eyes seemed to burn right through me—or perhaps through my pretensions.

She took a polished, black-surfaced mirror out of her purse and looked at her reflection. At least I thought that's what she was looking at, but maybe she was seeing something else.

She put the mirror face-down on the table. "I think we've done enough."

"You're ending the session?"

She nodded.

"Can I come back?"

She glanced at me, then looked away. "Perhaps. At any rate, you can try."

Puzzled again by the abrupt termination, I thanked her and stood up. As I opened the closet door, I looked back. The Seer sat motionless in the large room, staring intently at the mirror-topped table covered with cards. I closed the door.

The light went out.

Three

A week later I returned. I entered the bookstore and knocked on the closet door. A voice called out, "Come in."

Everything looked just the same. In fact, nothing had changed, not even the Seer's clothes. She was still sitting at the mirror-top table, which was still covered with its mirage of cards; her purse still dangled from the back of the Plexiglas chair.

"I'm glad you are still here," I said, with an unexpected sense of relief.

She welcomed me with a wry smile. "It was time for you to return."

"I feel like I never left. Or rather, I feel like I was only gone for a moment."

"There is no time but now," she reminded me. "And now is the time to continue."

"I have many questions to ask—"

She raised her hand imperiously. "Now is not the time." She touched her long, red-tipped finger to her lips, indicating I was to be silent.

I had learned it did no good to argue, so I sat down on my chair and drew a card, or a card drew me. I turned it over and saw an antler-crowned woman standing on a sled. I handed the card to the Seer.

"If I were you, and this were *my* card…." She began.

Playing the Elen of the Ways Card

I see before me a broad-shouldered woman wearing a headdress made of deer antlers—or perhaps the antlers spring directly from her head. I can't quite tell. Her body is swathed in a green velvet cloak, wrapped over a long red velvet gown. She stands on a sled pulled by a reindeer. There is something numinous about her.

"Who are you?" I ask in awe.

"I am Elen of the Ways, though some people call me Elen of the Roads."

She can see I am puzzled, so she continues. "I travel in dreams. I am the Guardian of the Paths, both in this realm and the next. I help people find their way, in this world and the next. There's not much difference, after all. The path leads through unbroken, although there is a checkpoint at the border."

"What are you doing here?" I ask.

"What are you doing here? It's you who drew the card, not me."

"You're right, of course," I reply politely. "Perhaps if you tell me more about yourself I'll have the answer."

She wrinkles her nose, amused, unaccustomed to being asked so many questions. "Some call me Elen of the Ways, some call me Elen or Helen of the Hosts, confusing me with a Welsh queen who married the Roman emperor Macsen Wledig. The legend goes that she appeared to him in a dream, and he could find no rest until he found this woman 'as beautiful and radiant as the sun.'"

Like a child being told a bedtime tale, I am enthralled. I sit down on the edge of the sled and look up at the towering, antlered figure. "How'd he find her?"

"He followed his dream back onto this mortal plane."

I look puzzled.

She rolls her doe-like eyes. "In other words, he found her by literally using the dreamscape as a map and mapping it onto his territory. Once found, Elen refused to marry him until he gave her the British Isles and built her several fortresses, promising to unite them with a network of roads. You can still find the remains of these trackways—some of which are in fact older than the Roman roads—in Wales. Many are marked by standing stones. They are called Sarn Helen."

The antler-headed woman shifts her stance and then continues, "Although I am often confused with Elen of the Hosts, I am not her. My lineage is much more ancient. I am the Guardian of the Ways, the Opener of the Path. I am Elen of the Pathways, both physical and not. I am Elen of the Dreamways, the Spirit Ways. Follow me and I will lead you on a journey that will take you farther than you have ever imagined."

I am filled with enthusiasm and, momentarily, with courage. I cry out excitedly, "Yes—yes! Take me with you!"

She looks down at me from her sled. "Where do you want to go? What Path do you want to follow?"

Shocked, I realize I have no answer. "I do not know."

She nods, her heavy antlers swaying with the movement of her head. "A wise reply. Most people think they know and are mistaken." She gestures with a generous hand. "Climb up beside me and we will begin our journey."

"To where?"

"Ah, that I cannot tell you."

"But aren't you Elen of the Ways, who guides people on the many Paths? How can we go somewhere if we don't know where we're going?"

"I am indeed your guide upon the Path, but as to the destination—that will have to be revealed."

She sees my hesitation and laughs, a strange, whinny-like snort. "Trust in my guidance, and you'll enjoy the journey. If not, well, that too will be revealed!"

I take her proffered hand and jump onto the sled in a leap of faith. She flicks the reins, and the reindeer leaps forward, dancing and prancing with delight. In no time at all we are flying over a deep-rutted track in a northern landscape, a bleak barren countryside spotted with blackened birch trees and stunted evergreens. In the distance, a small dot rapidly grows larger as we approach: it is a large, circular mound covered with stubby, winter grass. A circle of ancient standing stones surrounds it.

I expect Elen to steer around the mound, but instead she heads straight at it, at break-neck speed, urging the reindeer into a full-out run. A reclining megalith carved with a triple spiral blocks the entryway. Involuntarily I raise my hands to shield myself from the impending crash, but the reindeer jumps easily over the meter-high stone and we careen into a dark tunnel, the reindeer's hooves striking hard upon the smooth surface of the floor. Ahead of us, the stone-lined passage expands into a circular chamber. The reindeer skids to a halt and we behind her.

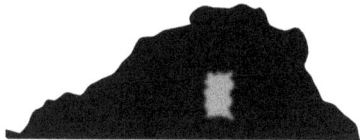

I take a deep breath and look around. "This mound seems much larger on the inside than the outside."

"Indeed it is."

The room is lit with torches. Red flames reflect off the glistening walls, which are dripping with condensed steam. In the middle of the chamber is a pit of bubbling mud. The reek of sulfur fills the air.

"Where are we? What kind of place is this?" I ask fearfully.

"We have entered the Hollow Hills, where size and time can be deceptive." Elen smiles at me and points with an antler tip: "That mud pit is for you."

"For me?"

"For you. We cannot go further on our journey until you cleanse and purify yourself."

Even where we stand, I can feel the heat radiating from the pool. "Surely you jest."

"It's a little late for second thoughts," she says with disapproval. "You should have had those before you hopped on board."

I protest, "I didn't know where we were going."

"We never do. Either you trust my guidance or you do not. I'm offering you an opportunity not many are afforded. What say you?"

I pause a moment, then reply, "I say what you have said: It's a little late for second thoughts. What do I need to do?" I ask, sounding braver than I feel.

"Take off your clothes and bathe."

Obediently, I strip off my clothes and fold them on a ledge along the wall. Then I hop and skip towards the pit, my bare feet burning as they touch the heated ground. I gently edge my way into the pool of steaming mud, gasping at the heat and choking on the smell. But soon the hot, gently bubbling fluid lulls me. Buoyed by the viscous liquid, I float upon my back. I enter a dreamlike state of total relaxation. Visions float before my eyes and disappear: animal shapes, landscapes, human forms.

After a while—I don't know if the time is short or long—I hear Elen calling me back. I splash upright and look around. Two dark, dwarf-like figures stand beside her, holding a large white cloth.

"Is that for me?"

She nods.

Dripping with mud, I walk over to the figures, expecting to be wiped clean. Instead, they wrap me round in a winding cloth, then lead me, hobbling, to a low-slung cot. They help me lie down, and soon I fall asleep, swaddled like a baby or shrouded like a corpse.

I begin to dream of a dark place, hidden deep in the Earth, where snakes slither and dogs roam, a place of healing, where knowledge is given to those who remember what they dream and make the proper sacrifice.

And then I dream of a very different place, a place beyond space and words and names and concepts, a place that fills me with immense longing.

Time passes—again I know not how long or short—and I awaken to a gentle humming sound, a cross between a wordless lullaby and buzzing bees. The two assistants have returned, and they hum as they unwrap me from my covering. I realize I still can't move: The dark brown mud has hardened into a carapace.

They reach into their tool belts and pull out small metal hammers. They strike, and shards of rock-hard mud scatter on the floor. They crack me open from my shell, and I emerge like a newborn chick from a shattered egg. My skin is pink and soft.

Elen looks at me with approval. "Did you have any dreams?"

I nod and start to speak.

"Hold the memories close, for first you must choose what you want to wear," Elen commands. "Think well. Your decision is laden with significance."

I see my old travel clothes laid out before me, but next to them is something else: a pair of loose leather pants and a jingle-fringed tunic with elaborate symbols painted on the front and arms. Without hesitation, I put on the pants and tunic, marveling at their softness. I trace the symbols with my fingers: a spiral, a five-pointed star, a crescent moon, a deer.

Elen smiles. "Now our real journey can begin," she says, and tilts her heavy-antlered head in my direction. She picks up an oval frame drum, decorated with strange designs, and starts beating a hypnotic rhythm with a spiral-incised antler. "Where do you want to travel?"

This time I know the answer. "I had a vision while I lay dozing on the cot. I saw a path before me, a bright path going from Earth into space, or perhaps to the Other World, or perhaps somewhere else. I was told it is Jacob's Ladder and that it leads to the Heavens. Can you take me there?"

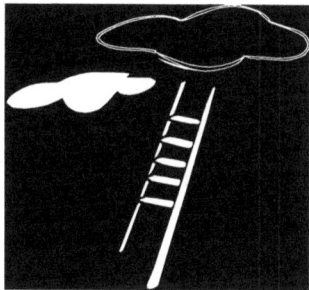

"I will, since you have passed the test, and because I can." She proclaimed proudly, "For I am Elen of the Ways, Elen of the Dreamways and the Hidden Paths. I will take you to Jacob's Ladder, because you passed the test and because I can. But climbing it is up to you."

I nod.

"First, however, you must learn to drive the reindeer."

The Seer placed the card down and sighed. "That's a good story, that! I remember those days as if they were yesterday."

"You do? What days?"

She gave herself a shake. "Following the long-distant Sarn Helen trackways in Wales, when I was younger. Much younger. Now, do you have any other questions?"

I laughed. "Of course I do! What's with the woman with the antlers? And the mud bath? And the dreams?"

"What do you think they mean?" She snorted. "Elen is right. You ask too many questions. First, you need to learn to drive the reindeer!"

"I know this much. It's a story of initiation and shamanic journeying. Of death and dying and being reborn."

"Not bad for a beginner."

I ignored her snide response. "I want to know what happens next."

"And so do I. So let's begin again, though not at the beginning." She picks up the card.

I stand beside Elen on the sled, confident and excited. At last, at last the day has come. I pat the dark-silver rump of the reindeer. I twitch the reins, and the reindeer starts trotting, her wide-spreading hooves padding gently on the ground. The air smells cold and harsh, and vapor rises from the reindeer's steamy breath and hangs above her frosted head.

The night is brilliant with falling stars, exploding distant galaxies, and nebulae spinning in the sky. The Milky Way pours itself across the heavens, and the Plow wheels around the Pole Star. The moon is but a curving splinter of herself, but I know she will return to fullness, as she always does, and then fade to darkness once again. The cycles continue, beyond our human reckoning.

Our path is clear although no milestones show the way. We ride in silence until we see a glittering iridescent beam of light before us. It looks like the Aurora

Borealis would look if it touched the Earth instead of dangling provocatively in the sky.

Elen points with her antlers. "There is your entrance to Jacob's Ladder. I'll take you to it, and then I'll wait till you return."

I nod, suddenly shivering with anticipation. We reach the spot. The shimmering, ever-shifting column of light touches the land and stretches up out of sight. I don't know if it comes from above or below—perhaps both at once in a never-ending, evolutionary and involutionary flow of up and down and up again. It looks as if it is in constant motion, as if I am looking at the movement of particles of light shifting through the spectrum. I wonder if it is a mirage. Can I really climb it to the stars?

As if in a dream, I step down from the sled, pat the reindeer on her velvety, ice-rimed nose, and walk toward the mesmerizing vision. I reach it and reach out, expecting to put my hands through the gossamer veil of multi-colored light—but much to my surprise, it is more solid than it looks.

I say a prayer of protection: "May the doors, and gates, and paths between the worlds be open to me—and may the doors, and gates, and paths of any who wish to do harm to me or those I love, be closed! May it be so."

Then, carefully, cautiously, I place my right foot on the flickering curtain of light and find a transparent step. I stretch out my hands to either side and find two invisible railings. I take another step and discover that

*the shimmering Aurora Borealis conceals a staircase.
Jacob's Ladder. I climb the stairs and disappear.*

The Seer stopped speaking.

I sat silently for a few minutes, contemplating what this might mean. Then I said, "I take it I had an initiation. A rebirth. Followed by a journey to the Cosmos. It was … amazing. I—it *was* I, not you?"

She nodded.

"I need time to understand how this relates to my question. Or maybe to understand what my question really is. Or what the real question is."

The Seer waited motionless. It was almost as if she didn't need to breathe.

At last I said, "I want you to teach me to 'read' the cards."

"Why?"

"I want to know what is happening when you read the cards. I want to understand what it all means—and what it has to do with my life."

"That's the second time you've asked. I'll think about it. But we've done enough for today."

"I'll see you same time, same place, next week?"

"Perhaps. You never know." She waved a dismissive hand, and I picked up my things and left.

Four

A week later I returned. I entered the bookstore and knocked on the closet door. A voice called out, "Come in."

✳

The Scribe held up his hand. "Wait! Let me catch up." He continued writing, then put down his pen. "I get the idea. Every time you go back to the bookstore the same thing happens at the start, right?"

I nodded.

"So I don't have to write it down, over and over. I can just write 'ibid.' That saves some effort." He sighed.

"Even though I'm an old hand at this, my fingers are starting to cramp." He massaged his hand and stretched his legs. "That's better." Then he frowned, worried. "I hope you don't think I'm complaining. It's a real honor and a privilege to be recording your story. The spirit is willing, but the flesh is weak—after all, I'm only human."

I smiled. "I could go slower, but that would simply make the telling longer."

"No, no—the pace is right. I just need to take some breaks and review my notes to make sure I didn't miss something." He glanced at the last few pages he had written, then looked up. "That's quite a story you're telling. Your Elen of the Ways is really something! I wish I could meet her."

"Perhaps you will. After all, she isn't *my* Elen of the Ways. You can call on her just as well as I can."

The Scribe looked uncomfortable. "I've never been into making offerings and worshipping deities, if you know what I mean. Some people really get into that, but not me."

"I know exactly what you mean. I've never been into devotional practices either. Remember, I was a skeptic, a 'dis-believer.'"

He waited for me to continue.

"However, over the years I've learned that there is guidance and support, and—for want of a better word—archetypal energies that are accessible. The way they appear to us depends on our personal histories and our cultural conditioning."

The Scribe nodded as he continued writing.

"You might have an experience of the numinous—of something from 'beyond'—and given who you are and how you grew up, you might identify it as an apparition of the Virgin Mary—or as a visitation from Isis or Demeter. And if deities aren't your thing, you might simply have an experience that fills you with awe or immense confusion."

The Scribe nodded again.

"For example, in India, many people bring offerings to images of an elephant-headed, pot-bellied god named Ganesha. They hope he will intervene for them. He's famous as a 'remover of obstacles.' Asian elephants can move huge tree trunks and carry heavy burdens, so they are indeed removers of obstacles."

The Scribe looked up from his notebook and smiled.

"Many devotees sincerely believe there is an elephant-headed god named Ganesha, and they experience his presence. Just as some people sincerely believe there is an antler-headed goddess named Elen of the Ways and think she has personally guided them on a journey.

"Maybe that doesn't work for you—it's not part of your experience or goes against your upbringing or your theology. If so, you can use these images as something to focus energy and intention, rather than as something to worship. You can ask 'Ganesha energy' for help to carry your burdens and remove blockages. You can ask 'Elen of the Ways energy' to show you the path forward."

"We're talking figuratively here, not literally?"

It was my turn to nod.

The Scribe asked, "Is that the same as imaginary? In other words, made up?"

I shook my head. "No, it's not made up. It's very real. It's imaginal, not imaginary. As you hear my story, I hope you'll understand the very significant difference." I took another sip of chai. "Now it's time to continue with my recitation, don't you agree?"

He nodded, his pen poised over his notebook.

✳

Everything looked just the same. In fact, nothing had changed, not even the Seer's clothes. She was still sitting at the mirror-top table, which was still covered with its mirage of cards; her black patent bag still dangled from the chair.

"I'm glad you are still here," I said, with an unexpected sense of relief.

She welcomed me with a smile. "You decided to return."

"I feel like I never left. Or rather, I feel like I was only gone for a moment."

"There is no time but now," she reminded me. Then, looking at me quizzically, she asked, "Why did you return?"

"I want you to teach me to read the cards."

"That's the third time you've asked. But I'm not sure I want to teach you, and I'm not sure you are ready to pay the price. However, I will take your request under advisement."

She took out her table mirror again. "See this mirror?" She said.

I nodded.

"See how it reflects?"

I nodded again.

"Look carefully. It is not a reversal of reality that you see. The right side of the 'you' in the mirror isn't your right side—it's your left. You raise your left hand, and the right hand of the 'you' in the mirror goes up. Correct?"

I nodded, puzzled.

"The mirror image is not a reflection of you from the mirror's perspective. The mirror switches front and back. It's like the impression made by a printing press or a rubber stamp. Your right hand in the mirror is actually your left, and your left hand in the mirror is actually your right. You understand that clearly?"

I nodded again, even though I didn't.

"A reflection is not the same as a reversal. Don't take anything for granted. Perhaps if you remember this, it will help you see through illusion into reality. Perhaps not." She smiled wryly. "And once you *do* see, you will be surprised to discover which is which."

She picked up a card seeming at random from the table. She handed it to me. "Look at it closely. What do you see?"

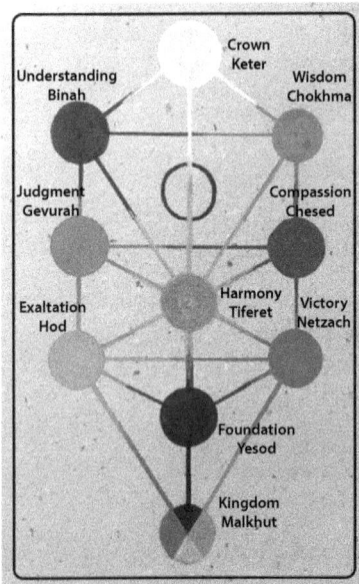

I had seen the design several times before. "It's a Kabbalist Tree of Life, surrounded by a black frame."

"Does the Tree face you, or are you seeing it from behind?"

I was puzzled. "How can I know?"

"Precisely. That's the point. How can you know?"

Now I was even more puzzled. "What does this have to do with reading the cards?"

She snorted in contempt. "If you can't get this straight, there's nothing I can teach you. Stop a moment and reflect. It's all about reflection."

Obviously, this was another test, and this one was clearly mine to pass or fail.

I held the card in my hand, examining the drawing.

"How much do you know about the Tree of Life?" She asked.

"Not much. I know that Jewish Kabbalah groups and Western esoteric mystery schools like the Golden Dawn use it to represent reality. At least I think that's what they do. Some of the Trees have lots of Hebrew writing on them, but this one doesn't."

"You're right. This Tree is the most well-known representation of the Tree of Life. It's one of many, by the way, all equally valid. It includes ten disks or spheres, called Sefirot. They are numbered from 1 at the top to 10 at the bottom. Number 1 is called Keter in Hebrew. It is also known as 'the Crown.' Number 10 is called Malkhut, also known as 'the Kingdom.' The Sefirot are arranged on three pillars, left, right, and middle. 22 paths flow between them. These paths are often associated with Tarot cards, but we won't get into that now."

I studied the drawing.

She continued, "Each Sefirah (that's the singular form of Sefirot) has specific attributes or qualities. Moving down from the Crown, I'll give you a very simplified, one-word description for each Sefirah." She pointed as she spoke. "This is Wisdom, next is Understanding, Mercy, Judgment, Harmony, Victory, Exaltation, Foundation, and, finally, at the bottom of the Tree, is the Kingdom—the materialized, physical world. Different schools of Kabbalah attribute different but related qualities to the Sefirot, but you get the idea."

"I think so. I see that some of the Sefirot are opposite each other on the left and right pillars and some are off-set in the middle. I presume that means something."

"Indeed it does. For example, Chesed, which you see here in the middle of the right-hand pillar, represents qualities like Loving Kindness, Grace, Mercy, and Compassion. Opposite Chesed, on the left-hand pillar, is Gevurah, which represents qualities like Judgment, Discernment, Strength, and Severity.

"You can see that the two balance each other, although either can easily get out of balance. There's a constant interplay between the side pillars and the center via the connecting paths—most of which pass through or connect to Tiferet—Harmony, Truth, and Beauty—in the center of the central pillar."

The drawing was beginning to make sense. "There's the outline of a circle in the center of the card, near the top of the middle pillar. You didn't mention that."

"That's Da'at. It has a special role, but I don't want to get into that now."

I examined the card. "Each disk has a different color."

She nodded. "Each Sefirah has many associations: colors, metals, planets, Hebrew names of God, gods and goddesses, angels and archangels. It can be very confusing. People spend their lives trying to understand the Tree of Life. I'm trying to keep it simple, but you need to understand enough about this diagram for us to work with it."

I nodded. "Ok, I think I get it."

"The Tree of Life diagram is like a map of reality. The Sefirot are the ten attributes or emanations through which God or the Divine reveals itself. These ten aspects of God descend into the increasing denseness of manifestation from the realms of the unmanifest. You might say, it's God's way of expressing God's self. Are you with me?"

"Maybe…. But why are you telling me all this?"

"Now we are getting to the crux of this exercise. We can visualize the Sefirot on our bodies and experience the energies directly. After all, we are the Tree of Life. That's why knowing which way the Tree of Life faces is important."

I frowned. "I don't see what difference it makes."

She sighed. "You do insist on making this difficult. Let me try to make this simple. Imagine that 'Kingdom' is placed at your feet. 'Foundation' is placed at your lower belly. 'Harmony,' by the way, is at your heart. And 'Crown' is above your head. Now: where is Mercy? On your left or on your right shoulder? And where is Judgment—on your left or on your right shoulder? Members of the Golden Dawn place Mercy on the left shoulder—but members of Jewish Kabbalist groups place Mercy on the right shoulder. Now do you get it?"

Suddenly I got it. The left pillar in the Tree of Life would be "placed" either on your left side or on your right side, depending on your point of view. Members of the Golden Dawn assumed that the observer was standing "in front" of the Tree—"face to face," so to speak—and reversed it to draw it on their body. The "right-hand" side of the drawing was visualized as being the "left-hand" side of the person.

But what if, in fact, you were actually looking at the *back* of the Tree, not the front? Then Mercy would be placed on your right side and Judgment on your left. The Seer's question was anything but trivial. She had asked me to determine whether I was looking at the Tree from the back or from the front. But how could I possibly know?

I turned the card over. On the back was an identical image, which did nothing to resolve the question.

The Seer tapped her foot upon the floor, her stiletto heels clicking loudly in the otherwise silent room. Her impatience was obvious.

I carefully formulated my answer. This was a test I could not afford to fail. "The answer is, it all depends on your perspective. Both are correct, and perhaps neither. The real Tree of Life isn't a flat image on a piece of paper. It's three-dimensional. The drawing is a two-dimensional representation of the nature of reality, which is beyond our comprehension. It's a map mistaken for the territory."

She nodded and her foot quit tapping.

Gaining confidence, I continued, "If I were to draw this image in another way—concentric circles, for example—the problem would disappear."

"Exactly!" She said, clapping her hands. "You begin to get the idea. By the way, there are practitioners who are certain which perspective is correct. Theirs! According to Jewish belief, humans cannot bear to look directly into the face of God. If I remember correctly, when Moses saw the Burning Bush, God turned its back so as not to annihilate Moses with the unbearable glory of its being. Since the Tree is an expression of God's Face, Jewish Kabbalists are sure they are seeing it from behind.

"But if you are a Western esoteric Qabalist, you are sure that you are looking at the front of the Tree. It is facing you, face to face. Naturally, each group is convinced the other is wrong. And then there are some Western mystery schools that have it both ways—you use one perspective when you are looking at a drawing of the Tree but the opposite when you are 'placing' it on yourself."

I smiled in relief. I had passed the test. "Why would the Western esotericists make that mistake, if mistake it is?"

"Ah, that's a difficult question. Perhaps they simply did not know better because, centuries ago, they learned their Kabbalah from Jewish books, not Jewish Kabbalists. Or perhaps they reversed it intentionally, since mirroring is a way to gain power and claim something as your own. Remember what I said about mirrors?"

This was all very interesting, but I was puzzled. "What does this have to do with 'reading' the cards?" I asked.

She sighed. "I can tell that teaching you will be a slow and lengthy process, one that will truly try my patience. Let me give you a hint. You think I am 'reading' the cards, correct?"

I nodded. Of course I did.

She leaned over the table toward me. "But what," she whispered intimately, her breath carrying the scent of wild honey fragrant with lavender, "What if the card is 'reading' *me?* You think I am 'seeing' into the story in the card—but what if the story is 'seeing' into me?"

Grasping the meaning behind her words, I had a sudden attack of vertigo. The room started to whirl around me like a spindle. I was in the middle of a conceptual earthquake that threatened to knock me off my feet.

"'The center cannot hold....'" She whispered.

My head was spinning. I swallowed hard against rising reflux. I closed my eyes and inhaled for four counts, held for seven, exhaled for eight counts. I repeated this four times. That helped. Slowly the gyrating world stabilized and came to rest.

I put my hands on the round table to steady myself. I glanced at the mirrored top and saw a haggard face staring back at me. Its eyes looked like those of a deer caught in headlights. Startled, I drew back, then realized the face in the mirror was my own.

The Seer patted my hand. This was the first time we had had physical contact. Her fingers on my skin felt like a static-electric charge. Like stroking velvet. Quickly she withdrew her hand.

"That's what happens when your paradigm shifts," she said. "Don't worry. You'll get used to it. Unless you want to quit? If so, there is no time like now, and now is the time, when we have barely begun." She cocked her head to one side and looked into me. "Although I think it may already be too late for you to quit."

I squinted at her through barely open eyes. "You're right. Once your worldview cracks, it's cracked. There's no putting the old one back together. You have to formulate a new one." I rubbed my aching head. "And to think, I thought I was lost before!"

"Just remember," she said, perhaps attempting to reassure me, "Reality is just a story we tell ourselves and sometimes share with others."

I contemplated the ambiguity of this statement.

She started to shuffle the cards, then her hands stopped moving. After a few moments, she asked, "Are you ready now to learn to read the cards?"

I was stunned. "Did I hear you right? You're really offering to teach me? I thought you said I had to pay a price."

"You just did. A change in paradigm. Though that is just the first instalment. The final price is yet to be determined. I have decided I am willing to teach you. Are you ready to learn?"

81

I closed my eyes and went deep within. I tried to listen to my inner guidance. Slowly, I replied, "Yes, but not yet. I thought I was ready but I'm not. I need time to process all I've experienced so far. Or at least, some of it. Then I will be ready to begin."

I waited anxiously for her response.

She nodded unperturbed. "In that case, we will begin the lesson after the next card."

I sighed with relief. She had accepted me on my terms.

✳

I looked at the Scribe. He seemed lost in thought, staring into space, his pen suspended above the page.

I asked, "Do you need another break?"

He shook his head. "I'm doing okay. I was just lost in thought. I really like that part about the mirror images and the reflections. It makes sense. If the Tree of Life is really three-dimensional, like reality is, you could walk around it, right? So how could there be only one way to look at it? There couldn't be!"

"You are a quick study. Much quicker than I was."

The Scribe continued, dreamily. "I'm wondering—what would the Tree of Life look like from the side? Or from the top? Or—from the inside?"

I smiled. "Make a 3-D model and you'll discover some very interesting things. By the way, you can draw the Tree of Life using eleven concentric circles— that's a way of looking at it from inside. Or outside."

The Scribe's eyes opened wide. "Wow. I wonder—is the Kingdom in the center and the Crown outside? Or the other way around? I mean, it makes a huge difference, doesn't it?"

"You are indeed a quick study." I moved my legs, which had fallen asleep, and took another sip of chai. "Ready to continue?"

"Ready when you are," he replied, licking the tip of his pen.

✳

I mixed the cards, and one separated from the rest like oil from water. I turned it over. I saw a picture of a large tree with strange hanging fruit, including the strangest fruit of all: a man hanging upside down. A serpent slithered between the tree's gnarled roots. The Seer reached out her hand and I gave her the card.

"Ah. Yggdrasil. The World Tree. I know it well. If I were you, and this were *my* card…."

Playing the Tree with the Hanging Man Card

The Hanging Man thinks aloud, "My foot is numb. The rope noose looped tight around my ankle has begun to bite into my flesh, cutting off circulation. My head hurts from hanging upside down for so many days. I've lost track of how many it's been. I think it must be eight now, or maybe nine. I am hungry and thirsty. My side hurts, where something I can't quite see is nibbling at my flesh. And there's also that self-inflicted spear wound, caused by the spear I made myself for myself. That hurts as well, a pain that throbs and throbs, matching my heartbeat. My foot used to throb, but now I feel nothing.

"If I'd known what I was getting myself into, I might have had second thoughts. In fact, I might never have decided to do this thing. What looked like a worthy quest now looks like a foolish undertaking.

"There are those who say I stop at nothing in my search for knowledge. They accuse me of obsession. Perhaps they are right. But what else is there to do with one's life, especially when one is a god?"

He licks his peeling, cracking lips. "Self-sacrifice is one thing, but martyrdom is something else. I wonder: Will I ever find what I seek? Will I ever be released? Sometimes I even wonder: Am I a traitor to my cause?"

He pauses, listening to a rustling sound that comes from far below. "A huge snake weaves its way among the roots of this great green ash tree. I hear it scratching itself against the thick, coarse roots, beginning to shed its skin. Some say the snake destroys the roots, but

I know better. It constantly regenerates itself and the Tree. But even so, the Tree and the snake cannot live forever. Nothing can. The dragon gnawing at the Tree's great roots, and the goats nibbling at its bark, and the stags eating its leaves will make sure of that."

The Hanging Man twists his head from side to side and looks around with his bright right eye. The left one is noted by its absence, for he plucked it out long ago.

Why, you wonder, would someone sacrifice his sight? You can ask the man hanging on the Tree.

"How did you lose your eye?" I ask. "Forgive me for the question. I mean no disrespect."

He answers firmly, his voice still strong though dry and husky from thirst. "I didn't 'lose' it, as you euphemistically put it. How could I 'lose' my eye? It was well attached. I tore it out and threw it in a well. I realized that although I had two good eyes, my vision was flawed and limited. I was blind to Truth.

"The offer was made, and I accepted it, to lose one eye to gain a deeper vision. It seemed a worthy sacrifice at the time, and so it has proven to be. Nothing of value is gained without a sacrifice. The greater the value, the greater the sacrifice."

Gaining courage, I ask another question. "Why are you hanging from this tree?"

"I have chosen to sacrifice myself for the greater good—much better than having someone else sacrifice me for their own purposes. In giving I receive; in letting go, I control my destiny."

"What is this tree you hang upon?"

"Its name is Yggdrasil, 'Odin's steed'—or maybe 'Odin's gallows,' depending on how you take the meaning. I hang here immobilized, sure enough, but I am confident the tree will be my steed to carry me to where I want to go."

"While you still hang here with a noose around your foot?"

"Of course. One doesn't have to be mobile to travel to another realm. Sometimes the only way forward is not to go anywhere. We spend too much time running away or running toward. Sometimes the only way to reach where we are heading is to enter into stillness, letting go of time, of space, of movement … and then we realize there is nowhere to go and nothing to do."

I think about that, but the words slip through my grasp. I ask a different question.

"Are you hanging from the Tree of Knowledge?"

"Although I seek a certain kind of knowledge, that is not the nature of this tree. Yggdrasil is the living tree that stretches from the depths of Matter through the Nine Worlds into the heights of Cosmos, where the stars are born. Its roots are fed by many streams and several wells, some earthly, some not so much. It was at *one of those that I partially lost my partial sight to gain a clearer way of seeing."*

I pause, struggling to formulate my questions.

"Does no one offer to help you?"

"No one else can do the work that I must do. No one can eat for you or breathe for you. And no one can make the sacrifice that you must make for yourself, of yourself."

"How can you gain what you seek, hanging by one leg from a tree?" I ask again.

"That is the Mystery, is it not? Perhaps I can't. We must wait and see. I admit this pose grows tedious, even for a god."

A chattering squirrel runs up the tree, carrying a message from the dragon below to the eagle at the top. I hear a commotion in the leaves. Two ravens start to "Kraa" loudly at each other. One drops a tiny piece of carrion that lands on the Hanging Man's face. He raises a hand and quickly wipes it off, grimacing at the smell.

I find another question. "What is it that you seek?"

He smiles, a cracked and tortured smile. "If only I knew...." He sighs. "How I long for a cup of mead!"

I hear a rhythmic whirring sound and see three women with spindles and a loom sitting among the massive tree roots. A brimming chalice sits beside them on the ground. "Perhaps they can help?" I ask.

He shakes his head. "Better not to know what future they are weaving, or how long is the thread they spin. No, no one can help. I must hang here until I find what I am seeking."

I leave the Hanging Man and begin to circumnavigate the tree. Suddenly I hear a shout—of pain or exultation I cannot tell—and I run back to see. The Hanging Man no longer hangs upon the tree. Instead, he is sitting on the ground, holding within his cupped hands a collection of dancing, glowing signs: the runes.

"Is this what you sought?" I call out eagerly.

"It is what I have received."

"Was this worth such a sacrifice?" I ask, my voice filled with doubt.

"Without the written word, my always-curious friend, you wouldn't be able to read or write this story."

The Seer replaced the card. "A very interesting card, wouldn't you agree?"

I pondered its meaning—its meaning to *me*. Was I willing to partially lose my vision, to lose my partial sight, so that I could truly see? What was I willing to give up for knowledge? What price was I willing to pay?

And even more important: What sacrifice was I willing to make for the greater good of humanity? I realized I didn't know. I'd never thought about self-sacrifice or about being of service to the greater good. I'd only thought about myself.

I wondered: Are these the important questions the Seer had alluded to?

Suddenly weary, I realized how long this visit had been.

"I think it's time for me to leave."

She looked up, her right eyebrow raised.

"I can't absorb any more. I need to process all that's happened."

She nodded.

"I'll return a week from now."

"What makes you think I'll be here?" She replied.

Startled, I said, "I just assumed you would be, since you've agreed to teach me."

"Be careful of assumptions. You never know. We'll have to wait and see."

I nodded and went out the door. The light went out.

Five

I had a very difficult week, filled with anxiety, confusion, and obsessive rumination.

✳

The Scribe stopped writing and looked up, perplexed. "I thought you were going to start the way you always do, by returning to the bookstore."

"This time was different. Let me continue."

"Sorry. Of course!"

✳

As I said, I had a terrible week, filled with confusion and anxiety. I thought I was going mad. My view of reality was crumbling and I needed help. I had thought I was lost before, but now I knew I was really lost. So I decided to go back to the used book store, hoping I could have an extra session with the Seer. But she wasn't there.

*

The Scribe stopped writing again. "She wasn't there?"

"More precisely, the used book store wasn't there."

"The used book store wasn't there?"

"That's right. At any rate, I couldn't find it. I retraced my steps several times, thinking perhaps I had simply mistaken the path through the maze of alleys and lanes. But I couldn't find it. It was very peculiar. After all, I had found my way there once a week without any problem. But when I tried to go there on a different day than the one agreed upon, I couldn't find the bookstore. At the time, I told myself that I was so confused, my connection with reality was so thoroughly shattered, that I simply didn't know where it was. Or where I was."

"What did you do?"

"What could I do? I waited until the appointed time and went to see the Seer."

"And?"

"This time, I had no problem finding the book-store."

"That's really weird."

"No weirder than many things that happened. On reflection, I realized it was necessary that I figure things out for myself and not rely on the Seer to make things right. That was something the Seer was trying to teach me. Relying on someone else to solve your problems—or validate your reality—or interpret your cards—is a dangerous thing."

The Scribe frowned. "But isn't that what a teacher's for?"

"Absolutely not. It's dangerous to give anyone that kind of power over you. Guidance and support are important, and a wise teacher can provide them when you lose your way or stumble. But there's a limit, a boundary, which should never be crossed—neither by the teacher nor the student. That way lies idol worship, and the temptations are as dangerous for the idol placed on the pedestal as for the worshipper." I shuddered. "But I'm sounding preachy. Let me return to storytelling. It's much more entertaining."

The scribe nodded and picked up his pen.

✳

After a very difficult week, I returned to the book-store. I knocked on the closet door. A voice called out, "Come in."

Everything looked just the same. In fact, nothing had changed, not even the Seer's clothes. She was still sitting at the mirror-top table, which was still covered with its mirage of cards; her black patent bag still dangled from the chair.

"I'm glad you are still here," I said, with an enormous sense of relief.

She welcomed me with a smile. "You decided to return."

"I feel like I never left. Or rather, I feel like I was only gone for a moment."

"There is no time but now," she reminded me. Then, looking at me quizzically, she asked, "Are you ready to begin?"

"I'm lost, totally lost. I'm in Nowhere Land, stuck between one reality and another. So yes, for sure, I am ready to learn to read the cards. Things can't get any worse."

She nodded. "We are all in Nowhere Land, for everywhere is nowhere, and nowhere is everywhere. You are just beginning to recognize the true nature of reality. Don't worry. With time and proper training, you'll learn to toggle back and forth."

With a shudder, I said, "I hope so. I really do."

I took my familiar place at the table.

She put her long fingers together, as if in prayer. "You are ready for your first lesson?"

I nodded resolutely.

She said wryly, "You won't regret it. Or perhaps you will. One never knows about these things."

I stirred the cards. One card rose to the top, like cream on milk. I looked. I saw a white space surrounded by a gold frame.

I handed it to her.

She stared at it for a moment. "This card is most unusual. Perhaps it will make the lesson easier, but perhaps not. We'll have to see."

She paused for a moment and put the card down on the table. "I will draw another card for guidance."

She wove her hands over the cards in a spiraling pattern. A card emerged to meet her swirling palms. She turned it over.

"Death. The Grim Repeater." She began. "If I were you, and this were *my* card...."

Playing the Grim Repeater card

The Grim Repeater repeats his wearisome task, wielding his razor-edged scythe across the ripened meadow. Mice scurry and rabbits flee before his relentless advance. Birds startle up and fly to nearby trees. A butterfly flutters too slowly and loses a wing, a beetle its head, a sunflower its petals. Half of a still-writhing garter snake lands on the severed grasses, and sweet-smelling blossoms topple to the ground, shorn from their stems. He tramples them all under his sharp, skeletal feet.

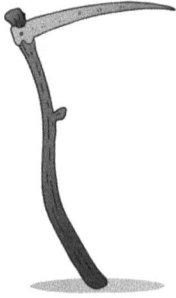

At last Death stops and looks around, putting down his grass-stained scythe. His seemingly random onslaught has sliced a labyrinth in the field. Pleased, he smiles grimly and surveys his work. A falcon spirals high in the sky, riding thermals, perhaps examining the design from a bird's-eye view.

A raven lands upon his bony shoulder and "Kraa's" in his bony ear.

Death smiles a toothy grin. "I'm glad you like it. I get so tired of dealing out destruction, I thought I'd be creative for a change."

He picks up a severed daffodil and sticks it between two upper ribs, where his heart would have been. He takes a whiff of the herbal scent born on the gentle, late afternoon breeze. "Ah, the smell of fresh-cut grass. I love it, don't you?"

The raven croaks, "Kraa."

He strokes its beak. "I'm glad I have you to talk to." He sighs. "It's not easy being Death. I'm always the bad guy, the one who causes everybody grief. Humans are the worst. They think if they ignore me I'll go away. They say, 'if I die,' not 'when,' and hide their dying relatives in hospitals so they can avoid meeting me firsthand. They are like ostriches sticking their heads in the sand.

"The cycle of Life and Death can never end. And I'm the one elected for the job. I drew the short stick, eons ago. I've tried to take time off, but nobody will agree to be my substitute. I've thought of going on strike, but I

know I'm indispensable. That's the good news and the bad."

He sighs resignedly. "Maybe I need to join a trade union."

The raven croaks, "Kraa-kraa-kraa!"

He pets the bird. "You understand and you appreciate me. Without death, you'd have no carrion to eat and nothing to feed your fledglings in the nest. Without death, the ecosystem would be clogged with too much life. Just imagine this overgrown field, if I didn't cut it down. If everything that ever lived were still alive…. Life feeds on death, not the other way around. It's part of Nature's cycle. The Cosmos births new stars from the material spewn out by dying stars in their death throes."

He looks at the sun beginning to set, and wearily picks up his scythe. It's time to get back to work.

I looked at the Seer uneasily. "This doesn't sound like a good card to get."

She seemed unperturbed. "Don't be so quick to judge."

"Death? Or, as he calls himself, the Grim Repeater? How is that *not* a bad card?" I exclaimed.

"Didn't you understand a thing he said? Life feeds off death. It's part of the natural cycle. From the moment you are born, you start to die."

"Exactly. More death. More ravens. And this time, the Grim Reaper—the Grim Repeater—himself!"

"Don't take it so literally. There are many kinds of death. The Sufis say, 'Die before death and resurrect now.'"

"They do?"

She nodded. "We have to die to the old so that we can embrace the new. Isn't that what you are doing? Dying to your old ways of understanding reality?"

"It feels more like a terminal illness than an accomplishment to be celebrated," I complained.

"Nobody said this would be easy." She continued, "This card is a powerful affirmation of our work together."

"You think so?"

"It shows you how deadly serious this training is and reminds you, at the same time, to not take it too seriously. After all, the Grim Repeater in the card has quite a sense of humor. Don't you feel some sympathy for him, condemned to always wield that scythe? No sick leave, no holidays?"

"I guess so," I said, doubtfully.

"Besides, what's so fearsome about death? If you knew it was just a 'change of state,' a kind of transformation, would you still be so afraid?"

"I suppose it's the finality of it all."

"Didn't you hear what the Grim Repeater said? Life and death are an endlessly repeating cycle. He didn't say, 'Death is the end of the road.' Or the end of the story. He said, 'The story continues.' The more you experience the other realms, the less you'll fear death."

"Promise?"

She looked surprisingly solemn. "I promise." Then, brusquely, she asked, "Now, are you *finally* ready to 'read' the cards?"

I shifted my weight on the hard, Plexiglas chair, trying to get comfortable. "I'm ready—and eager—to begin."

She peered unblinking into my eyes, as if trying to transmit something beyond words. "Here's what you must do. Set your intention to 'read' the card. Go within to that inner place of stillness and detachment—you know where it is. From this place of relaxed, focused concentration, look at the frame around the space on the card. Shift your attention to the space within the frame, memorizing it until you can see it with your eyes closed, until you see it reproduced exactly in your mind's eye."

I asked, puzzled, "The card I chose—or that chose me—has nothing on it. How can I 'read' a blank card?"

"You shall see what there is to see."

She handed me the card. I stared at it and concentrated, closing and opening my eyes.

"Do you have the image memorized?"

I nodded. "There's nothing except the gold frame to see, so that's easy."

"Now comes the interesting part. You enter into the picture on the card."

"I what?" I sputtered.

"Imagine the golden frame around the card becoming a door frame. It grows until it fills your visual space. You step inside the doorway. It's like crossing the threshold of a door that separates outside from in."

I shook my head. "I don't get it."

"It's easier once you get over the idea that it can't be done."

I asked suspiciously, "Isn't all this just imaginary?"

She rose from her chair and loomed over me, seeming to grow twice as large. "*Just* imaginary? That's like saying *just* your mind, or *just* life, or *just* coincidence." She sat down hard on her chair and quickly regained her composure and normal size. "The word 'imagination' has been so misused, subjected to such abuse—I suppose it's no wonder you don't understand the true significance of what we are about."

"You're right, I don't," I grumbled.

"The imaginal realm is as real as the world you think you live in when you are awake. When you dream, or when you die, or when you go on a shamanic journey or a guided vision—or have a waking dream—or when you 'read' a card—you are entering into the imaginal realm." She sighed. "I take it you've never heard of it."

"When you talk about 'imaginal,' I think of 'imaginary.' And next I think of Disneyland cartoons and computer games, and sci-fi movies."

"*The Matrix* got it almost right," she mused. "The imaginal realm is a kind of virtual reality, but what isn't? Do you think reality TV shows are real? Or a politician's promises? The artificers of games and movies create imaginary worlds, often using powerful archetypal images and mythic storylines for their own nefarious ends. You can get drawn into those imaginary worlds, but they are entirely different from the imaginal realm."

Leaning forward, she continued, "In fact, they are a perversion, for they supplant your own active imagination with a store-bought, artificial, ready-made surrogate. You don't need a video game or a TV screen to enter the imaginal realm. In fact, you can't get there if that's how you try to enter."

She spread her hands over the table and began to agitate the cards. "The imaginal realm is as real as this world but not as … solid. Things morph and shift easily because they are not as dense. You could say their vibrational state is higher.

"In these other realms—I have spoken as if there is only one, to make it simpler, but there are many and they often overlap—your body can change shape. You can encounter ancestors, swim like a fish, fly like a bird, shift locations and centuries in an instant. In some of these realms, the so-called dead continue living and learning. In other realms, you can journey entirely beyond form."

"Are you sure you aren't making this up?" I replied, defensively.

She looked angry for a moment, but then emitted that strange, barking laugh. "Ha! Me and many others who explore these realms in depth. Including Sufi mystics like Ibn Arabi, in the thirteenth century, and members of numerous contemporary esoteric and shamanic schools."

I bristled at her tone. "There's much I don't know, but there is also much I don't believe in, like ghosts and fairies and extra-terrestrial abductions. I'm not gullible. I don't take anything on faith."

"Of course you do." She laughed that strange, barking laugh again. "You take it on faith that this world you live in is real—is solid. That what you see is all there is. Don't you realize, nothing is what you think it is? This physical universe you think you live in, which you think is so solid, is 99.9999999% space—including your own body, which you think is solid but is actually a nearly empty, rapidly vibrating electromagnetic field."

I looked at her in shock.

"That's right. Ask any physicist. And do you know that atomic particles can be measured as soon as they are observed, but not before, because they aren't there to measure? Observers can never know both the true position and the velocity of a subatomic particle at the same time. And do you know that light is both a wave and a particle, depending on the intention of the observer? And that once-united particles maintain a 'quantum entanglement' and respond instantly to what happens to each other, even when they are separated by an enormous distance? And—and this is the most recent, cutting-edge science—some 'entangled' particles emerge from different locations and are still entangled. And don't even get me started on string theory or multiverses!"

I listened intently. Some of this I'd heard before, but I had never thought about its implications.

She tried again. "You think that this world is real, solid, material. But think again. Have you ever seen a thought? Or a feeling? Of course not! Does that mean they aren't 'real'?"

Gradually, I began to understand.

She saw my dawning awakening and nodded, encouragingly. "'Notice the Mystery, how everything is, but nobody knows what it really is. Feel the mystery, breathe the mystery, be the mystery.'"

I took a deep breath in and out, and then another.

She continued, "Everything is interconnected. Everything is part of the great 'what is,' and we can't even begin to imagine what that looks like. So relax. Enjoy the mystery!"

I began to contemplate the immense unknowability of it all. "Reality" was so much less limited than I had thought. So much more—amazing. The vision the Seer presented was dazzling and oddly reassuring. But only for a moment. Then it was just confusing, and strange, and unimaginable, and I retreated into fear.

She smiled reassuringly. "The imaginal realm is no more illusory than this world. It's just different and operates with different rules. There are places there that are just as real, if not more so, than places on this planet. Libraries, temples, and other telesms—'structures' or 'locations' in the imaginal realm—have been built up, maintained, and visited over millennia by members of different spiritual and esoteric groups.

"And there are numerous inhabitants—ghosts and spirits, gods and goddesses, transhuman beings, once-human entities, visitors from other dimensions, to name a few. Some good, some bad, some in disguise, some worthy of trust and others not so much. But I digress. My intention is to teach you how to 'read' the cards, not to give you a lesson in the nature of realities. Although, in fact, the former requires the latter."

"My head is reeling."

"It should be. But you'll get over it. With proper training, you'll learn to enter and exit the imaginal realms, using the gateways that work best for you. You have paid the price—a shift in paradigm—to enter in, and I have agreed to teach you. Now, let's take a moment to center ourselves, and then we will continue the lesson."

✷

The Scribe put down his pen. "This is really amazing. I knew a lot of this science stuff already, but it's one thing to read about it, another to hear you talk about what it meant to you." He looked embarrassed.

"I hope you don't mind my interrupting! It's just…. Wow."

I smiled. "In telling you my story, I remember how I felt all those years ago. That rollercoaster ride of shifting realities, of things that made no sense suddenly making more sense than anything ever had. So take your time to think about it. I'm going for a walk."

With an effort, I pulled my stiff body up to standing and strolled slowly down to the lake. I looked at the moon's reflection on the momentarily placid waters. A fish jumped, a frog leaped, and the silvery image morphed into strands of liquid moonlight rippling over the surface. Gradually, the lake became still again, and the moon regained its mirrored *doppelganger*.

How beautiful it all is, I thought, and how ephemeral. Everything changes. Always. I looked again at the full moon floating in the sky. It looked so rock-solid. But appearances are deceiving. The constantly shifting image in the water was a more accurate reflection of reality than the oh-so-solid-looking moon.

Still stiff but refreshed, I made my way back to the dune, where the scribe waited patiently for my return.

"Ready?"

"Whenever you are."

I took a moment to regain the thread. I had so many stories I could tell. "Where was I?"

"You were about to do your first card reading, a white card with a golden border."

✳

I looked at the card I held in my hands. I closed my eyes and breathed slowly and deeply, consciously entering into a still, centered state. I imagined the blank white space surrounded by its golden border. I opened my eyes and stared into the card, intentionally enlarging it.

"If this were *my* card," I said, "And it is...." Consciously, deliberately, I drew myself into the white space surrounded by the golden frame until it filled my visual field. I stepped over the threshold and in.

Playing the Blank White Card

I pause and look around.

I report back. "Everything is blinding bright white light."

I look down. Everything I see is white. In fact, there is nothing to see—it's white everywhere, wherever 'here' is. It's like being inside a cloud lit by a thousand megavolt spotlights.

"What do you see?" *The Seer asks, her voice coming from a great distance.*

"I told you. Nothing. Everything is white."

"Look around," the Seer advises. "Perhaps walk deeper in."

"Deeper in? I might get lost!" I reply nervously.

"You know where you came in. You have it memorized."

"But there's no path—there's nothing to see! Everything looks the same. It's all blinding bright white light."

She sighs. "All right then, turn around. Now what do you see?"

I look and there, behind me, only now it is in front of me, is what looks like a gilded proscenium arch, through which I see myself and the Seer, sitting at a round, mirror-top table. Panicking, I leap through the opening and return to the room, panting with effort and anxiety.

"How was that?" She asked.

I wiped sweat from my forehead with a shaking hand. "Not very good. There was nothing to see. I was enveloped in bright white light, and I was afraid I would lose my way. And then…." My voice trailed off to nothing.

"And then?"

With a rush of words, I blurted out what seemed impossible: "And then I looked out through the arch, or maybe in through the doorway, and we were sitting here at this table."

She replied calmly, "Where else would we be?"

"But —but—" I tried to take it in, to make sense of this topsy-turvy world, but I couldn't. I took a deep breath. "What do you mean?"

"Obviously, we are sitting here. And obviously, you ventured forth into another realm of consciousness and then returned. What's the problem?"

Petulantly, I complained, "The problem is, I don't understand any of this!"

"What did you expect to see when you looked back through the arch? An empty chair? That makes no sense at all."

"It doesn't?"

"Think for a moment, and still your fast-beating heart. You don't venture into the imaginal realms with your physical form. How could you? That stays behind, doing what it needs to do to keep your body alive, while a part of you, a more 'subtle' or astral body, goes on a journey. Eastern traditions say we have a physical body and seven 'subtle' or 'energy' bodies."

"That's what happened?" I asked, doubtfully.

"When you dream, does your physical body disappear from the bed, just because you are in the Land of Dreams? Of course not. It stays behind, snoring and dribbling on the pillowcase."

"Entering the imaginal realm is like entering into a dream?"

"To be precise, entering into a dream is entering into the imaginal realm. We dream this world, and something else dreams us."

Trying to make a joke, I said, "So, am I a person dreaming I am a butterfly, or am I a butterfly dreaming I am a person?"

"Who's to say?"

"That isn't reassuring," I protested.

She spread her hands across the cards, palms down, fingers stretching wide, in a gesture I had seen before. "Look, if you want reassurance, this isn't the place to come."

I exploded with pent-up fears and frustrations. "Of course I want reassurance! I came here with an important question about my life, and I want the cards to give me the answer!"

She was unperturbed. "Apparently you have an even more important question guiding you. It's led you on a quest to find your True Self—your True Nature—and the True Nature of Reality."

I let the words sink it.

"There is no turning back once the quest begins."

"Are you sure?"

"You can always say you've had enough and leave the quest, but I promise you, sooner or later, in this life or the next, you'll start the quest again."

I sighed and handed her the card. "If this were *your* card...."

Replaying the Blank White Card

Everything is white, pure white, the color of in-nocence, the color of all possibilities, the color of light before it separates into colors. Every-thing is filled with light, as if lit from within. I am in-side a shimmering cloud. I look at my body and cannot see it. There is nothing to see. I realize that I have no eyes with which to see, and yet I see light everywhere. There is nothing but light, light penetrating light.

I move my hands—or perhaps the memory of my hands—and I feel them move, but I see nothing. There is nothing to see and I have no eyes with which to see. I move my feet—or perhaps the memory of my feet—and I feel them move—or perhaps I only remember the feel-ing of them moving—or imagine what they would feel like if I had feet and if they moved—but I see nothing. There is nothing to see and I have no eyes with which to see. I sense other beings like me moving in the shim-mering whiteout. There is nothing to see and I have no eyes with which to see.

I stay in this state for a very long time or perhaps for just an instant, for in this place beyond space, time has no meaning. Or rather, the time is always now.

Gradually, I feel a subtle pull, a drawing-together that makes my insubstantial substance slightly more substantial. I recognize this feeling: It is the pull of the Past or maybe of the Possible, pulling my soul-stream back into the world of manifestation. I feel myself begin to flow downward, although in this place beyond space there is no up and down. Nonetheless, I sense a vector, a direction to my journey, which I think of as "down."

Gradually, or maybe rapidly, I descend through the planes of existence into the materialized, manifest Cosmos, and then from distant stars to nearby galaxies to a solar system and a vaguely familiar, blue-splashed planet rotating around an incandescent sun.

At last I lodge in a shadowy place of watery darkness. I am surrounded by gently sloshing fluid, encased within an opaque membrane. I feel a delicate, pulsing heart beating in rhythm with another, louder heart. The heart becomes my heart.

I am waiting to be born again.

We sat across the table from each other, looking down at the cards. At last I broke the silence.

"Were you and I in the same bright white place, or did I go somewhere and you go somewhere else?"

"Either can happen. It all depends on how focused the intention, how sharp and clear the imagery. This time, however, we were in the same light-filled place. You simply didn't go deep enough."

"I panicked."

"You did well enough for a first venture in."

"Thank you. I didn't think so."

She nodded.

"I have another question."

"Of course you do." She gave me a wry smile.

"Did I—or you—*really* come to Earth to be reborn?"

"That question is as ambiguous as the answer I will give. Yes and maybe. The answer depends in part on what you mean by 'I' and 'you.'"

I started to ask another question, but she raised her hands. "No. No more questions. It is better to experience these things than talk about them. Once you have gained enough proficiency in these other realms, the questions become irrelevant and the answers become obvious."

She pointed at the table. "Draw another card."

The card I chose, or the card that chose me, showed lightning hitting a burning tower. Two people were falling from the flame-licked windows.

The Seer commanded, "Prepare yourself, and enter in."

I breathed slowly and deeply, memorizing the card. A white frame. A grey tower with a crown dangling off the top. How weird. A black night sky with three grey clouds and 22 tear-like drops of flame. 22, like the paths on the Tree of Life. A lightning flash from right to left that strikes the burning top of the tower. Three windows, one with flames. Two people leaping or falling from the tower, one wearing red and blue, the other wearing blue and red. Both are falling face down, but one falls frontwards, one falls backwards. Below, a rocky precipice on which the burning tower stands.

I opened my eyes and closed them several times until the image was seared upon my inner vision. I began: "If this were *my* card, and it is...."

Playing the Burning Tower Card

I smell the fire raging through the tower, consuming everything in its wild rampage. The smoke has an acrid reek. I cover my nose and start to cough. My eyes fill with burning tears. I hear the screams of the two people falling from the tower. They have no other way to flee. There is no fire escape, no ladder leading down. I want to call out, "You have leapt to your certain death!" I want to ask them, "Are you brave or foolish?"

Why is there no one here to help?

I watch in horror as they plummet towards the ground so far below. It's like a nightmare I had once of endless falling, falling endlessly. I want to escape this dream inferno. I feel so helpless. There is nothing I can do except bear witness.

Sad beyond words, I turn away, not wanting to hear the sickening smash of flesh on stone, not wanting to see the blood splashing on the rocks.

113

I turn my back on the fire-bright scene. There before me is a white proscenium arch. I step through.

The Seer was watching me with her piercing, raven-black eyes.

"Well? How was that?"

I wiped my tearing eyes. I could still smell the stench of the fire. I sniffed my hands and clothes in a futile attempt to locate the source. I blew my nose, expecting to see soot and ash on the crumpled tissue, but it was clean. I was relieved there wasn't any blood.

"Horrible. A burning tower, people falling to their deaths. I felt so helpless. There was nothing I could do but watch."

"Sometimes the witness is the most important person in the scene. Do you have nothing more to report?"

"Yes. No." I searched for words. "I have a question. Did that really happen? And was I really there?"

She sighed. "Ah, always more questions. It might have happened, or perhaps it will."

"You mean, we can see into the future in the cards?"

"Not into 'the' future, but into 'a' future. Or better said, we can see into 'the possible.'"

I looked skeptical.

"Perhaps you will understand more easily if I talk about dreams. You've had more experience dreaming than 'reading' the cards."

I nodded.

"Remember, I have been teaching you about the imaginal realm. We enter an imaginal realm when we dream. We call it the Land of Dreams. It's as real as this physical world, in its own way. We also enter an imaginal realm when we 'read' the cards. These realms are not the same, although they overlap and interpenetrate. But we won't worry about the details now.

"You are asking about seeing the future—or, rather, the possible. In the dreamtime, we can enter into the time-stream at any point and see where it has led and where it might lead. Remember: the past isn't gone, it accumulates. By re-entering our dreams, we can potentially shift the trajectory of events, nudging them into a different story. Scientists talk about the power of the 'strange attractor' that pulls us towards some event or perhaps pulls some event towards us. If we are aware of what might happen, we can take steps to encourage a different outcome. With practice, you'll learn this is a very useful tool."

I nodded, thoughtfully. "I think I get it. Once a friend dreamt that she was driving on a narrow road, and a truck came barreling down the road, heading straight at her. She pulled sharply over to the right and drove off a cliff. She woke up in a sweat, relieved it was only a dream. A few days later, she was returning from a visit in the country, and she was driving on a narrow road. She realized that it looked similar to the one in her dream. Suddenly a truck came barreling down on her. Because of her dream, she recognized the scene and took a different evasive action. She braked hard and was able to stop before going over the edge of the cliff. That dream saved her life."

"Exactly. Often there is advance warning in our dreams. As she and you discovered, it doesn't mean the future event is determined or predetermined. It simply means it's possible."

"But don't you always say, 'The only time is now'?"

"And so it is. The time is *always* now, but that doesn't mean there isn't a 'past' accumulating and a so-called 'future' filled with possibilities. That's the time-stream. We exist on that cutting edge, pressing against the membrane that separates the past from the possible."

I had a sudden sense of vertigo as I felt myself pushing against the membrane, the weight of time behind me, nothing but possibilities before me, only an invisible barrier holding me in the here and now, keeping me from falling into—where? Nothingness? No time? I needed a moment to regain my equilibrium.

At last I responded. "So ... when we read the cards, we are entering the imaginal realm, where we have access to the stream of time. When I 'read' a card, I could be 'reading' something that happened or could happen in the future, that is, in the 'future possible.'"

"Indeed. And don't forget, just as in a dream, you could be 'reading' something symbolic, or metaphoric, or something to do with psychological or emotional issues that are seeking your attention. Or something even bigger—a 'Big Dream,' if you will, with archetypal resonance, sent from a Higher Source."

I thought that over. "I had a dream once that I was supposed to go to Girona, a city in Catalonia, Spain, and say prayers for the dead. I even saw the tombstones. But was I really supposed to go there and do that?" I looked intently at her. "How do you know which kind of dream it is? How do you know the right way to interpret the card or the dream?"

The Seer spread her hands over the cards in that now-familiar gesture. "You don't. There is no 'right' way. That's like asking, 'What's the right thing to make for dinner?' Remember: nothing is certain. Everything is in flux. Life is a complex tapestry, woven out of many strands. Some rise to the surface while others hide within the complicated design. As to interpretation, experience will help you gain discernment. Sometimes we wake up knowing a dream is important, but other times we can't be sure. Often, we don't know a dream was precognitive until it plays out in our 'real' life. You'll get a feel for it. Some cards, just like some dreams, seem more important than others."

"It sounds like a recipe for uncertainty," I protested.

"Instead of getting frustrated, enjoy the wealth of interpretations and learn to stay alert and conscious. I promise you, this will enrich your life."

I looked doubtful. She sighed, and continued, "For example, perhaps your dream about saying prayers for the dead was metaphoric, not literal. Perhaps it was telling you to remember your ancestors. Sometimes we are called to act upon our dreams but not in the obvious way."

117

I thought that over. "I see that now. I sometimes wondered whether I had missed an important opportunity by not going to Girona. But maybe all I had to do was remember the dead. My ancestors. None of whom, that I know of, ever lived in Spain."

"There are ancestors of blood and ancestors of spirit. But that's another discussion. Now let's get back to the cards. We've talked enough about dreams."

"One more question. Do the images in dreams and on the cards have a specific meaning? For example, does the tower 'stand' for something? And the lightning flash?"

Annoyed, she snapped, "Haven't you been listening to anything I've said? Or are you so blind you cannot see what is right in front of you? I will give you a clue. Images in the cards often have consensual meaning, but we also bring our own meaning to them. If you consult a popular symbol dictionary, you'll be told the meaning of a snake or a lost shoe, or a loose tooth. To Freud, a cigar was never just a cigar, a pencil was never just a pencil—it was always something phallic.

"These interpretations ignore the fact that it is *your* dream, your card, your reading. The answer is both/and. Yes, the objects in our dreams, and in these cards, may have some standard, culturally mediated meaning, and yes, they also have meanings specific to our own life experience."

"Say that again?"

"The standard modern Western interpretation of snakes is sexual, but serpents also represent life renewal, healing, and wisdom. In the healing temples dedicated to Asclepius, the Greek god of medicine, sacred snakes slithered through the dormitories. In the original story of the Garden of Eden, the snake was a bringer of wisdom—a powerful, positive image, not something associated with evil. Maybe you like snakes. Maybe you have a phobia about them. A snake appears in your dream, or in your card, and you bring your own experience to its interpretation."

"I get it," I replied, remembering something I had read. "Dragons in Western mythology are usually evil, fire-breathing creatures, guarding treasure in underground caves. But in East Asia, dragons are positive beasts and bring good luck and fertility. They're associated with water and the Heavens."

"Exactly."

Delighted at finally breaking through the fog of confusion, if only temporarily, I continued, "So there's a personal, a cultural, and a transpersonal—a mythic or archetypal—aspect to interpreting symbols and dreams—and the cards." Excited, I continued, "In Chinese culture, the color black is neutral, and white is associated with death. Brides wear red for good luck. In the West those associations are reversed."

"Exactly. We bring meaning to, and find meaning in, the cards." She takes the card from me. "Would you like me to 'read' it now?"

I nodded.

She began, "If this were *my* card…."

119

Replaying the Burning Tower Card

I watch the tower burn with intense excitement. Free! I am free at last! The tower had held me prisoner for far too long, so long I had forgotten I was a prisoner. I praise the sudden strike, the lightning bolt of Fate that has shattered my world and set me free. I never would have left the tower on my own. In fact, I'd even forgotten I was in this self-created prison.

I see two figures diving out the windows, opposite images of each other. One wears a crown, but like the crown atop the tower, it does nothing to protect him now as he plummets head down through the air. The other, cape flying behind him, seems to dive through the fire-lit night sky. Their eyes are open wide in shock, their hands raised in surprise. Perhaps this is the only way they can free themselves from their illusions: They must let go of everything and jump into the unknown. Or maybe they were pushed by unseen hands. I don't know if they will have an easy landing, but I am not concerned. This is a time for old ways and old ideas to crumble on the rock below, the Ground of Understanding.

A large gilded crown, tipped on its side, floats in the sky above the burning tower. What a ruse that was, a fake crown made of Fool's Gold, fooling me into thinking that my entrapment was worth the price. Again, I praise the lightning strike, the flames that now engulf the tower. It's time—high time—to return to Earth. I've lived too long in an ivory tower.

I bless the fire, the flames of transformation. The phoenix bird emolliates itself periodically, only to rise again from the ashes. May it be so for me, I pray.

She put the card face-down on the table.

"You gave a very different 'reading' than I," I observed, "But, I take it, both interpretations are correct."

"Both are possible and both are meaningful. To know which story is more relevant to you, it helps if the card is one of several in a single reading. Card readers often draw a specific number of cards and place them sequentially in a 'spread.' Each card has an additional significance depending on where it falls in the pattern. It might represent the past, the present, action to take or avoid, the outcome, impediment, support, spiritual or physical issues, and so on, depending on the type of spread.

"Looking at all the cards, the reader then asks, how do they relate to each other? In your case, we haven't done a spread because a more complex intention manifested at the very start. And I am a Seer, not just a card reader. But it's been obvious that there have been recurrent themes: death, sacrifice, and transformation."

I nodded slowly.

"You might also notice," The Seer added, "that these themes are manifesting from the imaginal realm into this material realm we call reality. In this world in which you live, you are going through a kind of death and transformation. You are sacrificing old beliefs and slowly embracing new ones. Or perhaps it's working the other way around, moving from manifest to Spirit."

She was right. I sat back in the chair with a big smile, feeling very pleased with myself. But then a sudden thought struck me like a lightning bolt.

"Wait a minute! There's something wrong with all of this, something that doesn't jibe."

She lifted her right eyebrow again. "That is?"

"Well, you told a very different story with the Tower card than I did."

"So?"

"And every time I have given you a card, you have said, 'If I were you, and this were my card….'"

"And?"

"And then you've done a reading. And several times I've asked if the person in the story was me or you—for example, who passed the test?—but you didn't give a straight answer. If I understand what you are now telling me, I would read the card one way if it were my card, but you would read it another way if it were your card. Correct?"

She tilted her head like a curious bird but said nothing.

I continued. "In other words, you'd bring your life history and your personal symbols into the reading, not mine."

She waited quietly, unmoving. At last she replied, "What's your point?"

"Which is it? Have you been reading my story in the cards or your own?"

She laughed that barking laugh again. "We had this discussion once before, but apparently you have forgotten. Or perhaps you were not ready to understand. Don't worry, there's been no deceit. I have not misled you, substituting my story for yours. I have been reading the cards for you, not to you. I have been your substitute. That's why I am a Seer. I have learned the discipline of being your 'stand-in.' When I read the Tower card, you'll remember, I did not begin by saying, 'If I were you and this were my card,' as I had with other cards you gave me. Instead, I read it as my own."

"Ah." I felt a bit embarrassed. "I apologize for doubting you."

"No need. The question shows you are following my explanations and seeing where they lead. That is good. Not everyone you meet—in this realm or any other—is worthy of your trust. It is important to be cautious."

"Not trustworthy?"

"It's true. Not everyone is trustworthy in this world or the other realms."

"What do you mean?"

"Besides the obvious examples of fake fortune tellers and misguided channelers in this materialized world?

123

Some of the beings you meet in the imaginal realm are not what they appear. They may present themselves as someone you know or admire, Beethoven, or Jesus, or Dr. John Dee, or your dead grandmother, but that doesn't mean that's who or what they are. Their intentions may be benign or otherwise."

"That's a sobering thought."

"It is. It's easy to be intoxicated with the excitement of meeting famous people or long-departed loved ones, but always remember it is extremely important to be observant and skeptical. Always practice discernment. The imaginal realms are like places on this more physical plane. There are risky neighborhoods where it's not wise to walk at night without protection, and there are pleasant neighborhoods where friends gather to share a meal and exchange information. Part of the learning process is discerning how to judge."

"So it's not just 'fun and games'?"

"Never. Entering these imaginal realms is serious business. Having good boundaries is a necessity. To avoid 'bleed-through'—similar to when a particularly vivid night-dream 'bleeds through' into your waking day—it is important to open and close the gateways to the realms that you are visiting. You don't want to bring back unwanted guests."

"I see."

She leaned forward. "Don't worry. If you are reasonably well balanced and well grounded, no harm should come. Intention is important, and focus. Consciousness-changing drugs aren't necessary; in fact, they are counterproductive to what we are doing. And always remember, like attracts like. We draw to us what we resonate with. Energy flows where we place our attention. If you are ego-driven and seek power over others, dark forces will be drawn to you. And then, you might be unpleasantly surprised to learn who will have power over whom."

I shivered involuntarily. "I have another question."

"Of course you do. You always do."

I ignored the comment. "You said we weren't using a spread to read the cards, correct?"

"That should be obvious. We are drawing them one by one and replacing them in the pile."

"So, isn't this a kind of random walk? And the cards are showing up by chance?"

"Not at all. Rather than a random walk, we are on a 'walkabout.' A rite of passage, a pilgrimage, a quest mediated by the cards. Australian Aborigines follow 'songlines' laid down in the Dreamtime. We follow the stories in the cards. We may not know where we are going, but there is guidance in every step, with every card you draw. There is guidance whenever we ask, and even when we don't. Chance has nothing to do with it."

"Says who!" I blurted out.

"You are both stubborn and ignorant!" She shot back. "*Why* was I singing your praises just a few minutes ago!" Exasperated, she continued, "Look, you don't have to believe a word I say. The imaginal realms exist, whether you believe in them or not. Everything is interconnected, whether you believe it or not. More than a millennium ago—long before quantum physics was a gleam in Einstein's eye—the Hua Yin School of Buddhism described Indra's Net: an invisible, infinite net that spreads across the universe, that *is* the universe. At every node there is a glittering, multi-faceted jewel that reflects all the others. *Everything really is connected.*

"Indra's Net is something like 'the interdependent web of all existence' that your ecologists talk about, but it's on a cosmic scale. That's how those entangled particles can be entangled. How often must I repeat myself?"

She took a deep breath and let it out slowly. "Sorry for the harangue. I was acting out of character."

I took a deep breath as well. "I apologize for responded the way I did. Sometimes these ideas come at me so thick and fast that I react without thinking. I suppose I feel threatened. My old ways of thinking get triggered and I forget what I have learned."

Somewhat embarrassed, I continued, "I may be stubborn and ignorant, but I am teachable. Thank you for your patience. I've come a long way with you. I just don't want to lose my way or find I was misled."

She looked mollified. "You will lose your way, and you will find it again. Remember: 'Not all who wander are lost.' I think we've had enough lesson for today."

"I agree. I'll go home and try to integrate all this paradigm-shifting information."

"That would be a good idea. You have a lot to practice and learn on your own."

Surprised, I asked, "What can I learn on my own?"

"You can gradually begin to explore the imaginal realms, using the safeguards and cautions I've been teaching you. Beyond that, the more mythology, epic literature, and symbolism you know, the richer your readings will be. Extensive knowledge of the cultural and transpersonal associations in the cards will enable you to explore the deeper reality hidden beneath appearances. That way, you can 'read' a more complex, more fully resonant story."

"I know some mythology but not much. Mostly what I know I remember from my childhood. I was fascinated by fairytales, Greek mythology, Arthurian legends, that kind of thing. I think I lived in a make-believe world. Or maybe that was the real world, the imaginal realm. At any rate, I left those interests behind long ago. I couldn't see the point. They didn't relate to my 'real' life. Now I hear you say that in fact they do. They are just as 'real' in their own way." I smiled at the thought of reconnecting with my youthful interests. "Same time next week?"

"If I am here, and you are here. You never know. But perhaps we'll meet before then, in your daytime or maybe in your night-time dreams."

*

The Scribe stopped writing. "I gotta take a break. That was so intense. I mean—when you two started shouting at each other—I wasn't sure what was going to happen next."

"Now I can smile about it, but then it was frightening. Or rather, I was frightened, distrustful, suspicious. I suddenly felt like I was a puppet on a string. As you can see, my 'dying to the old' ways of thinking was neither easy nor quick. It was more like a series of intense earthquakes followed by lots of aftershocks."

The Scribe looked at me with admiration. "But you persevered."

I nodded. "I felt like I had no choice. I can see now, in telling my story, that hidden inside my desperation was a tiny spark of optimism and hope. I wasn't willing to give up." I took a sip of chai. "I guess my guardian angels were watching over me."

The Scribe looked startled. "I thought you were a dis-believer."

"There comes a time…. But that is another story. Shall we continue?"

He sharpened his pen and prepared to write.

Six

A week later I returned. I entered the book-store and knocked on the closet door. A voice called out, "Come in."

Everything looked just the same. In fact, nothing had changed, not even the Seer's clothes. She was still sitting at the mirror-top table, which was still covered with its mirage of cards; her purse still dangled from the Plexiglas chair.

"I'm glad you are still here," I said, with an unexpected sense of relief.

She welcomed me with a smile. "You decided to return."

"I feel like I never left. Or rather, I feel like I was only gone for a moment."

"There is no time but now," she reminded me. Then, looking at me quizzically, she asked, "Are you ready to begin?"

Anxiously, I reported, "I've had another rough week. Everything I thought I knew about reality is wrong. Or at any rate, shifting."

"The Spanish writer Calderón de la Barca wrote a play entitled *Life is a Dream*. You are discovering the truth of that."

I nodded, unhappily.

She continued, "The Taoist philosopher Lao-tzu wrote, 'Life is a series of natural and spontaneous changes. Don't resist them; that only creates sorrow. Let reality be reality. Let things flow naturally forward in whatever way they like.'"

"You've read Lao-tzu? I'm surprised."

If she was annoyed, she didn't show it. "I've read Plato as well. In *The Republic*, Socrates makes a significant point with the Allegory of the Cave. He teaches that most humans live in a dark cave, chained to illusion, seeing only shadows that they think are reality. That was true in ancient Greece, and it is true now. The toxic, so-called scientific materialist worldview—which is Newtonian and dreadfully outdated—encourages people to stay in the cave and mistake shadows for reality. Most people believe they live purposeless lives in a meaningless world. No wonder there is such rampant greed and such horrific environmental destruction. It's driven by desperation."

"You're quite philosophical today. Did something happen since I last was here?"

"Of course. Something always happens." She shrugged. "There is so much to teach—lifetimes of knowledge to impart. I try to stay 'on topic,' but sometimes the bigger picture calls and I succumb."

I waited, curious as to what would happen next.

She hesitated for a moment, then declared, "I'm going to start our session with a reading. I had a different intention, but now I sense this is the way we must begin."

She gestured at the table and I began the now-familiar routine, stirring the variegated cards until one stuck like glue to my fingertips. I looked: Nine large standing stones surround a mound-covered dolmen, its stone entrance open and dark. A full moon rises behind the tip of one of the megaliths.

She took the card. "If I were you, and this were *my* card…."

Playing the Dancing at the Dolmen Card

Istride up the path, passing through the narrow gap between two trees, one covered with white blossoms, one heavy with red berries. My leather sandals chafe against my feet, and the coarse dark wool of my robe scratches my skin. A heavy white cord wraps three times around my waist and ties in an upright, single-loop bow. Its long, knotted ends slap against my thighs with every step I take.

I look up and see the full moon already rising. Soon I hear drumming and a low, murmuring chant. I was unexpectedly delayed, and now I must hasten to the ceremony that has begun without me. I am panting now, hurrying up the moonlit path that meanders to the top of the hill. I see six dark rounded mounds silhoetted against the sky. Robed dancers circle around the central dolmen in a slow, rhythmic pattern.

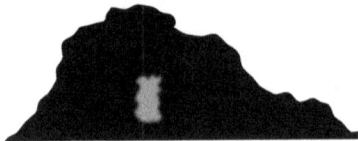

Soon I join the people dancing within the ring of standing stones that surrounds the mound-covered dolmen. We dance a simple circle dance, hands joined, arms held high, feet moving one way and then the other, our bodies twisting right to left and back again. I look to see who stands beside me, but their faces, like mine, are shrouded within woolen cowls.

In front of the entrance to the dolmen a cloaked, antler-headed being stands, human or other I cannot tell. He, or perhaps she, beats a hypnotic rhythm on an oval, skin-headed drum, using a polished piece of antler as a beater. A crackling fire blazes, constrained within a circle of river stones, and the smell of burning sage and pine fills the air.

We circle round, singing as the moon rises and the stars dim. We turn and turn in a widening and then narrowing gyre until—at last—the drumming stops abruptly. We halt exactly where we stand.

For a moment, even the stars pause in their cycles, and the moon waits poised above the standing stone. Then the antler-headed drummer beckons me with the beater stick.

In a gesture of acknowledgement, I cross my hands across my chest and bow. Then I walk slowly sunwise around the circle until I reach the drummer, who stands beside the entrance to the dolmen. I bow again. I take off my sandals and place them beside the stone doorway. I feel the prickly stubs of grass beneath my feet.

The drummer puts down the drum and picks up an elaborately carved vessel. I am given its contents to drink. The liquid burns as bright and hot as the fire in the circle of stones.

The antler-headed being pulls me closer and draws a pattern on my forehead—with hand or antler, with blood or soot or dye, I cannot tell. Then it presses down on the top of my head, muttering words I can't quite discern in a language I have never heard. Standing so close, I smell its breath, laden with the scent of herbs and berries. I have received my blessing.

The drummer points to a rope-tied bundle of branches that lies on the ground beside the fire. I pick it up and hold its uneven end against the flames. It catches, sending sparks that sprinkle the air like starflakes, singeing my woolen robe.

I bow again, this time to my companions in the circle, and they bow deeply in response. Then I turn and enter the tomb-dark dolmen, bending low as I crawl through the constricted corridor. The torch light flick-

ers, and shapes appear and disappear on the uneven stones that line the passage. A face, a skull, a bird. Something scurries across the wall—a lizard, perhaps, or maybe something else. I hear a slithering behind me as I crawl, but I do not turn to look.

The corridor opens into a large, corbelled chamber, tall enough for me to stand. Three small side-chambers lead off from it, each partly blocked off from the central chamber by a knee-high lintel stone. A metal hook awaits my burning torch.

A voice whispers in my ear: "You must choose your proper place." I look around but see no one. I am not surprised, for this is a place where the veil is thin between the worlds. I nod, though there is no one here to see me nod. I say a silent prayer, set my intention, and begin to spin, arms stretching out wide on either side, trying to sense which place is my proper place. My feet beat a steady syncopated pattern on the floor as I twirl. Soon, one chamber draws me to it like a magnet draws a lump of iron.

I step over the lintel stone and crouch inside the chamber. Carefully, I examine my surroundings. The rear wall is opposite the entrance to the dolmen. Twice a year at the equinox, when day and night are equal in length, the rising sun penetrates the lengthy corridor and momentary brightens this, the deepest, most distant chamber. It strikes the rear wall, which is covered with deep-incised designs—flower petals and zigzags, stars and suns, shields and moons. I trace the patterns with my fingers as the torch sputters out.

I am left in darkness.

The Seer put down the card.

I commented, "You've left the story only half-told."

"Have I now? How do you know it's only half-told?"

I frowned, puzzled. "It's obvious, isn't it?"

"Not necessarily." She continued, "There have been other cards we've left before the end and you did not object. There must be something different with this card." She thought a moment and then exclaimed, "Ha! It's obvious. This must have happened in one of your past lives. That's how you know!"

"One of my past lives?" I replied, flabbergasted.

"You heard me. One of your past lives."

"One of my past lives?"

"You are repeating yourself. Again. Here—" She handed me the card. "Finish reading your card. It's clear that it is yours to read."

I looked at the card and focused first on the frame around the drawing of the standing stones, the dolmen, and the rising moon. Gradually, the drawing expanded and I stepped through.

Continuing Playing the Dancing at the Dolmen Card

*I*t is dark and still—well, almost still. Something is slithering around on the ground and something scampers across the wall beside me. Something else flutters through the air above my head. I cringe

135

involuntarily, crouching lower in the chamber. I brush away a spider and wipe a cobweb from my face.

The air carries the flinty smell of darkness and dust and something else.

Beneath my bare feet, I feel the cold, smooth ground, worn smooth by millennia of use. I feel the rough stone walls beneath my questing hands, carved with intricate designs by my distant, ancient ancestors.

It is an honor given to few to be here at this time, the time of the full moon, the time of harvest. The antler-headed being chose me. I don't know why.

I know I'm supposed to do something here, but I don't know what. All my preparation—the years of training, of discipline, of ceremony—have primed me for this moment, yet I am not prepared. Or rather, I know what to do but not what will happen. How can you prepare for the unknowable?

With an effort, I remember what I know how to do, and I center myself, honoring the seven directions. First, the East, the direction of air and life and new beginnings, the arrow shot into the sky, the white of smoke and morning mist. Then the South, the direction of fire and light and fullness of adulthood and hot midsummer days, the upright rod to lean upon, the red of flame. Then the West, the direction of water and love and the wisdom of mature old age, the cup that runneth over with compassion, the blue of deep ocean. And then the North, the direction of Earth and law, destruction and regeneration, the hidden stone and the shield, the black of night sky and of inner knowing.

I honor the direction Above, the Cosmos that showers its spiritual energy upon me and surrounds me. I honor the direction Below, the Earth that nourishes me and supports me and holds me close. And last of all, I honor the direction Within.

I honor the ancestors of flesh and spirit who support me in this work, who hold me up and push me forward from behind, who have preserved these teachings through millennia of change and challenge. And I honor my companions, those who go before me and stand beside me and accompany me on my journey.

And then I chant three sacred vowel sounds three times, and I enter into stillness. My breath slows, my attention turns inward, seeking that Void that is both everywhere and nowhere. Time passes, though I know not how long, for time has no meaning here.

Gradually I become aware of a faint glow emanating from the eight-petal carving on the rear wall. I place my right hand on it—and I disappear into the Light.

After a time, I knew not how long, I handed the Seer the card. She waited in stillness.

I felt as if I were returning from a great distance. At last I said, "When I touched one of the carvings, I disappeared into pure white light. The kind of light we both saw in the blank card. Only, this time it was different, or maybe the light was the same but I was different. Instead of feeling anxious, I felt the light envelop me in a deep, compassionate presence. I felt at peace. A 'peace that passeth understanding.'"

I wiped my sweaty forehead with a tissue. It came away smudged with something that resembled soot. I looked at it in shock. The Seer watched me, unmoving as a stone.

✳

The Scribe stopped writing and his notebook slid off his lap. In a hushed voice, he asked, "That happened? That really happened?"

I nodded. "It really did. I learned later that such 'happenings' are rare, but they do occur. Some Indian saints have made their reputations on 'bringing through' material from other realms, or by materializing objects in this realm."

"I bet you were shocked."

"I was indeed. But now, can I continue with the story, before I lose the thread?"

"Of course—of course! I can hardly wait to hear what happened next!"

✳

"It was real. I was really there." I looked again at the sooty tissue. Seeing was believing. I whispered, almost as a confession, "I can no longer doubt that this happened in a past life. My past life."

"You sound surprised."

"I am. I never really believed in past lives."

She started to speak, paused as if reconsidering, then asked, "Do you know you have a soul?"

Nonplussed, I replied, "Why are you asking me if I have a soul? What's that got to do with this?"

"I didn't ask you if you have a soul. I asked you whether you *know* you have a soul."

Did I know I have a soul? Why was she asking that, I wondered, head reeling from the Seer's unsettling question.

She continued, "Without a soul, you couldn't have past lives."

No soul, no past lives? Past lives, soul; no past lives, no soul…. I let myself think back to the card reading, and I could taste the air and feel the cold stones—and I began once again to disappear into that all-encompassing, compassionate, pure white light. I was held in the arms of Love.

We sat in silence: I, suddenly drawn down deep within myself or perhaps completely outside of myself; she, waiting patiently for my return.

"Don't answer yet. Look within. What do you notice? Is there more to you than your sensing, thinking, perceiving, feeling self?"

In that poignant stillness, pregnant with possibility, I heard an inner voice whisper, "I Am that I Am.

I Am here. I exist as a soul-stream that has no beginning and no end."

There were goose-bumps on my arms, and I knew that Truth was speaking to me.

She must have heard my inner voice, because she suddenly leaned across the table, taking my hands in hers. Again I felt that odd electric shock.

I whispered, "What is this that I sense within?"

"You can give it many names. The Psyche. The Soul. The Larger Self. They are all subtly different, but this isn't a course in theology, so choose the name that you prefer."

"What does it mean to know I have a soul?" I asked, filled with wonder at this unexpected revelation.

"Knowing you have a soul has many consequences. You know beyond any doubt that there is significance in what you do. There is purpose in your existence. Your life isn't like a candle flame that gets snuffed out. Poof. The end. Your life isn't pointless, a random bit of chance, a game, something meaningless to pass the time until death. There is life after life, an endless—or almost endless—spiral of possibility. Surely you're beginning to see that now, to understand?"

I nodded slowly, realizing—I was suddenly brutally honest with myself—that I'd been acting "as if" what the Seer had been teaching about reality was real. But in fact I'd been holding back, not allowing this new way of seeing the world to expand my vision. Even though I'd been deeply shaken and felt my worldview breaking apart, I'd somehow tried to patch it up, to hold it all together. I had said that once my worldview was cracked, it was cracked, but the truth was, I'd been terrified to enter fully into this expanded view of reality. I'd been trying to patch the crack.

I admitted as much. "You know the saying, 'fake it until you make it'? I suppose that's what I've been doing. Except I wasn't *really* trying to make it. I was faking it. I was holding all I've been learning at arm's length, waiting until I felt more comfortable, readier to change."

"The time is always now," she said. "Now is the time to let go, to surrender. Otherwise, this life you're living is a waste of time. My time, as well as yours."

I looked down at our entwined hands, her fingers tingling and vibrant, mine cold and damp with anxiety. She was right. The only time is now.

I shivered, then replied, "I'm ready to make that leap of faith and claim my soul."

She held up a cautioning hand. "Don't do it out of faith, do it out of gnosis. Inner knowing. Look within and know that something exists beyond your mind, your thoughts, your feelings, your sensations. Something exists beyond your Limited Self and behind all your perceptions—something that doesn't end with death. Something that has had many lives and will have many more. And that's your soul."

I closed my eyes and breathed slowly, entering into that still place within. I finally got it. I really did.

She patted my hands and leaned back in her chair. "It's liberating to realize you don't have to do it all or get it all right this time around. After all, since you've had a past life, you'll obviously have a future one as well!"

We sat in companionable silence for a while, and I mulled over all I have learned. I began to feel deeply relaxed, as if I was letting go of an inner tension I hadn't known I held. I could feel a fundamental shift occurring, almost—it was hard to describe—as if reality was coming into sharper focus and I was seeing clearly for the very first time. I remembered a line from a song, "I was blind, but now I see...." I wondered if this was what Tiresias, or Isaac the Blind, or Odin had seen with their inner vision.

I waited eagerly, with childlike curiosity, wondering what would happen next.

Thoughtfully, the Seer put her fingertips together and peered into the open triangle, as if trying to see something. She said, "Don't forget, there are lost souls, and there is also such a thing as soul loss. But I think we should leave that discussion for another time."

A question occurred to me. "Is it possible that a soul can remember it has been reborn?"

"Of course, but only if it is an advanced soul. This happens more often in the East, where people believe in reincarnation. Or, to be more precise, it doesn't happen more often there, but people accept it as a fact and children aren't taught to hide the truth. There's a tradition in Jewish Kabbalah that souls return again and again, and after enough 'returns,' they begin to remember a little bit of their past lives. At least some do. And then, eventually, these more advanced, or 'older' souls, can choose whether to return or not. And many choose to return and be of service. This is similar to the Buddhist Bodhisattva concept."

Thoughtfully, I said, "I have a friend who seems to know an unusual amount of secret stuff about ancient Jewish history. He's even hinted that in a past life he was the famous medieval Spanish Kabbalist Nachmanides. I never took him seriously, but now I wonder."

The Seer looked into space before replying. "There are several possibilities. Your friend may have a powerful 'inner contact' that says he is Nachmanides. Your friend may think he is Nachmanides, that is, the soul of Nachmanides reborn in modern times. Or, your friend may be deluded." She shivered. "It happens, surprisingly often. Now, let's get back to the work at hand."

I wasn't ready to change the subject. "Is it possible that I lived here in a previous life, and that's what drew me here, to you and this used book store?"

"That would be one explanation." She smiled mysteriously. "Another explanation is that you were being given guidance by your Higher Self for your soul's development. Guidance that would, if you said 'yes,' enable you to learn about the true nature of reality. Both or neither could be true. These events are always over-determined. Now, let's get back to the cards."

She spread her hands over the tabletop and the cards began to swirl. I reached into the mix and two cards rose to meet my outstretched fingers.

"Two cards. That's very interesting," she observed. "Which shall we read first?"

One card dropped face up in front of me. "That one, I presume."

I saw a large, imposing building, a cross between the British Museum and the New York Public Library. I couldn't tell which it was since the image changed appearance while I looked at it.

"Shall you go first or I?"

"I'll start," I said, eager to begin.

She smiled approvingly.

"If this were *my* card—and it is...."

Playing the Library Card

I walk up seven wide, marble steps to the massive wooden doors of the building, framed by two immense columns. The stairs are concave with wear. Centuries or perhaps millennia of opening and closing the heavy doors has worn two curving tracks into the wide stone landing. I wonder if I will need to ring a doorbell or know a password, but as I approach, the doors soundlessly swing open and I walk in. But there seems to be a shimmering veil over the interior, and I cannot see beyond the entryway.

A guardian sits at a graffiti-carved school desk to the left of the door. He has the head of an elephant and a chubby chest adorned with necklaces; bright silk pants cover his ample thighs. His large ears twitch, responsive to every noise, and he rubs the right one with his sensitive, flexible, pink-tipped trunk. He is writing in a notebook with a broken tusk—his own—its once-white ivory yellowed from use. He hears me enter and looks up.

"Welcome to The Library," he trumpets, in a surprisingly high-pitched voice. "However, you can only enter if you leave something of value behind."

I look at what I carry: a bag of books, my cellphone, and a bottle of water.

He points at the books. "That bag of books will do. Best to leave behind what you think you know." I give him the bag and he gives me a numbered claim check in exchange: #31415926535897.

"Don't lose the claim check," he warns. "You might need it later. Now remember: no photographs, and silence is the rule. And turn off your cellphone for the duration of your stay."

He watches while I do so.

"And leave your water bottle as well. No food or drinks allowed." Then he gestures with his wonderfully expressive trunk. "Now you can enter."

With a wave of his hand, the veil disappears. I am standing in the atrium of a huge, two-level room. Elaborate geometric designs cover the distant, vaulted ceiling, and the floor is paved with alternating black and *white tiles. Rows of tall dark wooden shelves stacked with books and manuscripts fill both sides of the hall. Old-fashioned writing desks and chairs are scattered down the center aisle, some empty, some occupied.*

Curious, I begin to explore the main level, walking slowly up and down "the stacks," seeing titles in many languages, most of them unknown. Soon I realize that I am not alone. A white polar bear stands on its hind legs pawing through a book; an owl perches on the top of a shelf, engrossed in reading the small pamphlet it holds between its wings. Insubstantial phantasms flit in and out among the shelves. I wonder if they are characters in novels, or long-dead authors still attached to their publications. Several green-skinned beings, extremely tall and thin, dressed in iridescent robes, mutter something I interpret as "Excuse me" as they brush through me. I wonder if they come from outer space—or from some other dimension.

I continue to reconnoiter, walking down the central aisle. I try not to disturb the readers at their desks, but I gasp when I see a familiar face: William Butler Yeats is sitting at a library table, writing poetry or perhaps a play.

Gathering my courage, I walk up to him and say, "Excuse me."

He looks up with a frown; I have disturbed his concentration.

"I apologize for interrupting you, sir, but I have to tell you, your writing means so much to me! The brilliant imagery—the mind-shifting concepts—you have

inspired me in my own writing efforts, though of course they can't compare."

He looks at me in silence, so wise and tired and sad. I want to cheer him up, so I recite a line from one of his poems: "The center cannot hold/..."

That seems to make him sadder. "I agree," he says. "It cannot and it does not. I spent my life trying to make it otherwise, but there it is. Sometimes I wonder whether words can ever be found to 'knit the world back together.' That's what I strive for, but it gets more difficult with every passing year as the rough beast slouches toward Bethlehem."

I protest, "Only words can knit the world back together!"

"You're trying to encourage me," he says with a wry smile.

"And encourage myself as well," I admit.

He nods thoughtfully and returns to his writing. I walk on.

The hall seemed spacious when I entered, but now it seems even larger. I notice many more levels and doors that open into additional rooms. At the foot of a spiral wrought-iron staircase is a sign pointing up the stairs to "Akashic Records." Curious, I start to climb the flight of steps, but something makes me hesitate and I turn back. I'll leave further exploring for another day, when I know what I want to learn.

I turn the card face-down.

"Well done," the Seer said. "You're gaining more confidence with every card you read. Well done indeed."

I smiled, pleased with her praise. "I enjoyed that experience, I must admit. But I have some questions."

"Of course you have. You always do."

"Well, to start with, where did I go? And next—"

"One question at a time. First. You entered a well-established 'telesm,' a structure that exists in the imaginal realm and has existed for eons. It is frequently visited. You can find all sorts of information there, as you have begun to discover."

"So it's really a real place?"

"Are we back to that again? So soon?" She sighed. "Sometimes you sound like a broken record. Or rather, a recording that gets stuck in the same groove, over and over. Is it a 'real' place? It all depends on what you mean by 'real.' In some ways, it is more real than your neighborhood library. It has certainly been around for much longer. It is less 'substantial,' less materialized, shall we say, but no less real.

"You might say we are in a different location on the Tree of Life, somewhere above the lowest, most manifest Sefirah, which is Malkhut, 'the Kingdom.' Perhaps we are in Tiferet, the central Sefirah associated with harmony, beauty, and balance. All the other Sefirot are connected through Tiferet.

"Or, taking a different perspective, you might say we are in a different one of the Four Worlds, no longer

148

in the lowest World of Action but somewhere in the World of Formation."

I was confused. "I remember the diagram of the Tree of Life, but I don't remember anything about the Four Worlds."

"I over-simplified when I described the Tree of Life before. It also is a representation of what are called The Four Worlds: Emanation, Creation, Formation, and Action." With a flick of her fingers she materialized another card. "This is another way of describing the creation of the Universe, starting from nothing and ending up with physical reality as we experience it. The Four Worlds are different 'levels,' but they overlap and interact, and they co-exist in time and space."

I sighed. "I'm not sure that helps."

"Just remember: The map is not the territory."

I asked a different question. "Who or what are the beings that I met there?"

"Well, obviously, you are not the only one who visits The Library. It has been a popular meeting place for many creatures, from many dimensions, for many eons."

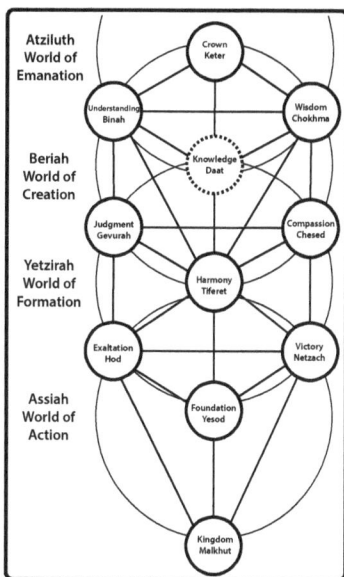

"I think I recognized the elephant at the desk. That's Ganesha, isn't it? The Hindu deity that wrote down *The Mahabharata* with his broken-off tusk?"

"That's right."

✳

Suddenly the Scribe started to cough and sputter. I reached over to pat him on the back.

"Thanks. That's much better."

"What happened?"

"I just swallowed something wrong. I'm okay now."

"Shall we continue?"

"Ready when you are."

✳

"So the gods are real?" I asked. "They really exist?"

"Again, it depends on what you mean by 'real.' Visible in this material realm? Rarely. Although sometimes they can be seen because they have been helped to briefly manifest by powerful practitioners and potent rites. And sometimes they manifest themselves if the need is great. That's why you hear of Marian apparitions, for example."

"But—"

The Seer interrupted impatiently. "Why on Earth would you think the gods were just a 'figment of the imagination'? By now you should know better. More correctly phrased, they are inhabitants of imaginal realms."

I rush on. "And W.B. Yeats? Did I *really* meet him?"

"That's more difficult to judge. You might have seen an aspect of his soul-stream that continues to exist nearly 100 years after he died. Some souls move quickly on, but others take their time."

"You mean, I really saw someone who has passed on?"

"Don't be so surprised! Where do you think the living go, after they die? They 'pass on,' as you so euphemistically put it, into another realm. A realm of life after death. Or better said, life after life. Remember, the soul doesn't die. So where does it go?"

"I really talked with the soul of W.B. Yeats?"

"I didn't say that. You might have, or you might not. It might have been a different entity disguised as someone you would want to meet."

"You mean he was an imposter?"

"I didn't say it was or wasn't. Not every spirit you meet is who or what it says it is. Shakespeare, or Mary Magdalene, or Socrates—think about it. Why would they want to hang around and talk to us? They have better things to do on their soul's journey! But then again, perhaps they have something important to impart and find someone worthy of imparting to."

She paused, then continued, "That's true for deities as well. The elephant-headed god you saw was probably not Ganesha. Gods tend to abide in another realm, closer to the Source, and few humans can experience them in their fullness without going mad or blind or dying. You probably saw a spirit taking on the guise of Ganesha, somewhat like an actor playing a part." She smiled. "He is a most appropriate doorkeeper for The Library, don't you think?"

I was inexplicably troubled. I didn't care if Ganesha was a spirit doing an impression of the deity, but I *did* care if I had talked with the "real" Yeats. "How can I tell if I really met the dead poet?"

"By asking him, or it, questions like, 'Who are you?' And by practicing discernment."

I must have looked very disappointed, because the Seer added, "Look, only you can judge the value of your exchange with this being who said it was W.B. Yeats. Did it feel genuine or somehow 'off'? Was the exchange meaningful or banal? Were you energized or drained? And so on. Even in our consensual reality, in this manifest plane of existence, not everyone is who they say they are, and even if they are, not everything they say has value."

Thoughtfully, I said, "I think I'm beginning to get it. Bit by bit."

"Practice, practice, practice. That's the only way. Trust, but don't take anything on faith. There's an Arabic saying, 'Trust in God but tie up your camel.' You understand?"

I nodded.

"Practicing discernment is not optional. It's mandatory. Now, would you like me to read the card?"

"Of course. I take it your reading will be different."

"I've said you need to use your judgment, but don't prejudge. Let's wait and see. If this were *my* card...."

Replaying the Library Card

I approach The Library, climbing up the wide, worn marble steps to the door. Two sculpted, flame-breathing dragons twist and twine on the heavy wood door. When I reach the wide landing at the top, the dragons suddenly come alive and challenge me, slithering out of the door and fanning their sooty wings.

"What do you want here?" Growls the rough, smoke-laden voice of the dragon on the left, while he flexes his talons.

"Why do you come here?" Hisses the dragon on the right, ominously twitching her long, barbed, scaly tail.

I have come prepared. "I seek knowledge to be of service to the Highest Good," I reply firmly.

They confer a moment. "Yessss," says one in a sibilant whisper. "Enter," says the other in a throaty rumble. They slide back into the door, and the door slowly opens. I have passed the first test.

I enter into a broad, expanding space that reminds me of an Escher drawing. Staircases lead up and down *in seemingly impossible ways; foreground and background interchange. The walls seem to shimmer, as if made of flickering light, not solid stone.*

A child-size figure suddenly appears beside me and trustingly reaches up its delicate hand to mine. It looks like my idea of an elf, or of some tiny faery creature. I take its offered hand.

"I'm here to guide you, if you'd like," the creature says.

I nod. "I'm grateful. Where do we begin?"

It waves a tiny hand towards the room. "This is the most accessible room, of course. It's filled with books and records, things you recognize."

I look around and see galleries of books piled upon more galleries, levels and levels extending up to the roof—which, I now realize, is black and covered with stars. Stars that move while I watch, circling around a central point.

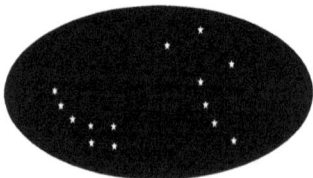

"There is much more to see, of course. It all depends on what you want to know."

Thoughtfully, I reply, "I want to gain knowledge in order to be of service to the Highest Good."

The elfin figure laughs, an oddly ominous giggle. "Now, that's a hard one! How are we to know what serves the Highest Good?"

"Perhaps I ask too much?" I ask, doubtfully.

154

"Or over-reach your very limited abilities. Your Ego has fooled you once again, giving you an inflated notion of yourself."

Could it be? I pause and ponder, deeply discouraged. I feel deflated, drained of energy. Suddenly, I think: Perhaps I'm being led astray.

"Who are you?" I ask, suspiciously, staring at the seemingly innocent little being.

No reply.

"Who or what are you really?" I drop the creature's hand and demand an answer.

The charming elfin figure shifts from foot to foot and suddenly disappears in a puff of smoke. A moment later, a beautiful ethereal being, shimmering with light, appears.

"That was wise of you," it says. "You have passed the second test. I have come to guide you through these Halls of Learning so you may be of service to the Highest Good. But first you must answer my question."

I wait patiently.

The Being of Light asks, "Who are you, really?"

I laugh, but then become quite still. Who am I really? Slowly, I reply, "I do not have an answer to your question. Perhaps that is what I really need to know."

"It is with self-knowledge that true service begins."

"Can I learn that here?" I ask. "And will you be my guide?"

The luminous figure nods again. "Of course. The Library is a repository of knowledge of all kinds, gathered together since the beginning of Time. This knowledge is more than information written in books or stored in digital files or coded tapestries. It is knowledge of the Nature of Reality. The Library is a place where Wisdom can be deepened and Understanding expanded."

My guide gestures, and a twirling, three-dimensional Tree of Life with ten sparkling Sefirot and one hidden one appears before me. The complex geometric figure spins around its central axis.

"Many who come here explore The Library at the level of the Lower Worlds, seeking and finding relatively concrete answers to their questions. They seek information, and there is nothing wrong with that. Others come to explore The Library at a higher level, closer to the Source, where Wisdom and Understanding abide. Is that what you are looking for?"

I am trembling with excitement and anticipation. "Yes—that's what I seek, though I didn't realize it before."

"Such a quest is lengthy, if not endless, and will take you many lives."

I take a deep breath and slowly let it out. I reply, "Then we had best begin."

My guide replies, "You already have."

The Seer put down the card and closed her eyes, lost in thought. At last she opened them and looked around, as if trying to remember where she was. Her raven eyes remained unfocused.

"Well," I said with false cheerfulness, eager to break the silence, "That was quite a different reading from mine, wasn't it?"

She didn't reply.

I tried again. "I have some questions."

That brought a smile to her strangely solemn face.

I barged on. "First, I understand that this reading is another affirmation of the soul-stream, of souls continuing through many lives, correct?"

"Correct."

"And that these 'places'—these 'spaces' that we visit in the cards—exist in many realms, many levels or 'worlds.' And that the imaginal realms are varied and overlap and interconnect. Correct?"

She nodded.

"And that there are guides that come to help us, right?"

"Yes."

"I remember you said there is always guidance if we ask, and even if we don't. And you said it was important to check out whether a being is what or who it says it is. Now I see that we also must be careful even with a guide that offers to help, like the elfin creature. It could have misguided you. It almost did."

"Exactly."

"I have one more question, and this is a big one." I paused, dramatically. "Were you surprised by what happened?"

She turned the card over and looked at the morphing image of The Library. "Yes."

Time passed and she made no move to speak.

Again I broke the silence. "Remember, there is another card to read. I drew two at once." I picked up the other card and turned it over. I saw four overlapping Kabbalah-style Trees of Life, forming a vertical, ladder-like design.

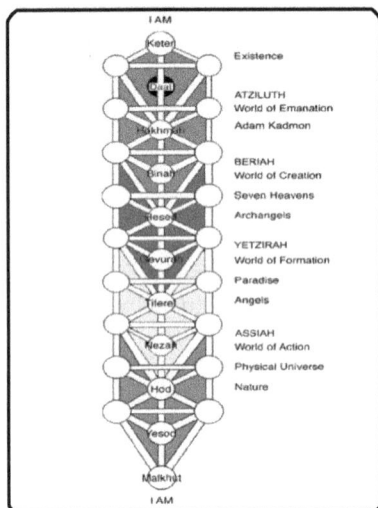

I AM
Keter
Existence
Adam
ATZILUTH
World of Emanation
Adam Kadmon
Hokhmah
BERIAH
World of Creation
Seven Heavens
Binah
Archangels
Hesed
YETZIRAH
World of Formation
Paradise
Gevurah
Angels
Tiferet
ASSIAH
World of Action
Physical Universe
Netzah
Nature
Hod
Yesod
Malkhut
I AM

As if returning from a great distance, the Seer slowly reached out her hand and took the card. Her eyes regained their focus. "How appropriate. You were asking me about different levels of reality. This card is a Kabbalist diagram called Jacob's Ladder. It is perfect for your next instruction."

"What luck!"

She frowned. "Luck, my friend, has nothing to do with it. It's synchronicity. Everything is interrelated. Remember Indra's Net? You can picture it as innumerable interconnected filaments of energy. Some of them have more 'affinity' to or 'association' with us, and we notice them more, or maybe because of this they are stronger and brighter.

"Synchronicity is like this thread of connection, like the thread Ariadne left for Theseus or the luminous thread the spider-woman gave you in 'The Well with the Staircase' card. There are other explanations, but these are as good as any."

"I remember, then I forget."

"No matter. With time, you will remember to remember. Now, let us examine this card."

Reading the Jacob's Ladder Card

She showed me the card, and I saw a complex glyph of interpenetrating Trees of Life in different colors. Numerous labels complicated the image.

"I've seen drawings of the Tree of Life before, but I've never seen anything like this."

"I'm not surprised. Jacob's Ladder was a central image in medieval Jewish Kabbalah, especially in the important thirteenth-century Spanish Kabbalist schools. But it was gradually forgotten, or perhaps it was intentionally hidden away, and the 'standard' single Tree of Life glyph supplanted it. The central importance of Jacob's Ladder was rediscovered in the 1970s by a Kabbalist based in London."

I sat back in my chair for a moment. "In other words, these ideas come and go in popularity?"

"Just like other ideas come and go."

"So why should I believe them?"

"You shouldn't. You shouldn't believe or disbelieve. You should work with them and see where they lead you. According to some Kabbalists, this diagram shows the true and hidden nature of the universe. We will use it as a teaching, not a reading, card. At least to begin with."

'But wait—" I suddenly realized I was very confused. "Isn't Jacob's Ladder that shimmering pathway from Earth to Heaven that I climbed in the journey with Elen of the Ways?"

"That's one way of experiencing it, but this is another. Different perspectives, remember? This card shows Jacob's Ladder as a glyph made of four interpenetrating Trees of Life, each with its own set of ten Sephirot. And each level, so to speak, is associated with one of the Four Worlds we talked about earlier. Imagine overlapping circles surrounding the overlapping Trees. The top circle is the World of Emanation, followed by, as we progress 'down' the Ladder, the World of Creation or Spirit, followed by the World of Formation or Psyche, and then, at the bottom, the World of Expression or Action. Although we talk as if these are different worlds, you can see that there is a continuous flow."

I tried to decipher the image.

She continued, "In addition, remember that the Four Worlds can be mapped onto each individual Tree."

My head was spinning. "Sounds like you are describing a fractal universe."

"Because it is."

"This is a map, right, not the territory?"

"Right."

I looked at the card again. "Four Trees, Four Worlds. Interpenetrating."

"Actually, you'll notice that there's a fifth Tree in the central pillar."

I pleaded, "Can you make this simpler?"

"I'll try. The diagram represents the flow of energy from the first moment of the Big Bang (which wasn't big and didn't bang) 'down' into manifestation. Remember Einstein's formula, $E=mc^2$? Matter and energy transform into each other."

"I'm not sure I get this."

"Think of energy—vibration—gradually slowing down and coalescing until it becomes form, like water vapor solidifying into ice. The reverse can also happen, of course. The flaming wick of a candle converts solid wax into light and incandescent gases."

"I get it. In the beginning, there was only vibration. 'In the beginning was the Word.'"

"Exactly. The Word, after all, is vibration. The Sanskrit phrase 'Nada Brahma' means that the world is made of sound. Jewish Kabbalah teaches that God created the universe using the 22 Hebrew letters—the same Hebrew letters written on the 22 paths on the Tree of Life. Kabbalists meditate with these letters, visualizing them, permutating them, chanting them aloud because, of course, the letters represent sounds. But that's another topic, too much to go into today. Perhaps some other time...."

*

The Scribe stopped writing. "Uh, I think I need another break. This is getting really complicated and I don't want to lose my focus and get it wrong."

"It is complicated. I agree. And yet—it's also simple. Energy becomes matter, and matter becomes energy. $E=mc^2$. Everything is always transforming. Physicists describe it one way, Kabbalists another. It's a matter of perspective."

I looked at the sky, thinking I was beginning to see a faint glimmer, or the faintest hint of a glimmer, of dawn on the horizon. "We're getting towards the end. I told you my story would be as long as the night but no longer."

The Scribe sighed, "The truth is, I'm getting a little tired. Not that your story is boring—it's fascinating! I really don't want it to ever end. I just need a little break." The Scribe stood up and stretched, then settled back against the dune. "Ready when you are."

✳

The Seer continued. "Let's bring this back to Jacob's Ladder. In the beginning is vibration. Actually, before that was nothing, but that's not shown on the Ladder. And then, gradually or rapidly, depending on your perspective, the vibrations slow down and 'fall' down the Ladder from the World of Emanation, until they reach the bottom of the lowest level, the World of Action. That's the manifest, physical world where we live. Or think we live. Most of the time."

"What existed before the World of Emanation?"

"Ah, you ask hard questions. According to Kabbalists, in the beginning there is God, nothing but God. But God wants to experience itself—which requires something external. In order for God to know God's self, God has to separate from itself. So this Ayin, this 'Transcendent No-thing-ness,' withdraws part of itself and creates Ayin Sof, 'the Absolute.' It creates a 'space' or 'womb' known as the tzimtzum or contraction. Into this space God breathes light, endless light, called Ayin Sof Or. And from this comes Emanation, the beginning of Creation."

"Not sure I buy that."

163

"Whether you do or not is irrelevant. You might notice, however, that this explanation makes just as much sense—and is pretty much the same idea—as the Big Bang. In fact, it tries to explain what happened before the Big Bang. A colleague of mine refers to it as 'the Void of Un-being, out of which all Being comes.'"

I asked, "As we move up and down Jacob's Ladder, are we moving back and forth from Unity to Separation, from Oneness to diversity?"

"You could say that," she replied.

"Is this like Enlightenment or Samadhi?"

"Well, that's a very complex topic. It all depends on how high you go up the Ladder. And moving up the Ladder is a very difficult task indeed."

"This is getting too abstract for me."

"Remember, this is a map, not the territory. And like any map, it is more or less accurate, depending on how it is projected, what the mapmakers considered to be significant, what they placed at the center, and so on. The map gives the mind something to do. And like any good map, you can 'map' all kinds of things onto it—including political systems, body parts, planets, psychological development, personal relationships, Hebrew Bible personages, and even Star Trek characters. What I've described to you is very simplified, perhaps over-simplified."

"There are angels in this system, right?"

She nodded. "Discarnate humans, angelic beings, and faeries tend to be found in the lower level of The World of Formation, the Second World from the bottom. Archangels exist in the next higher World, the World of Spirit or Creation. But it's more complicated than that."

"I was afraid of that," I sighed. "This seems so 'mental.'"

The Seer nodded. "There is a lot to learn."

"Why bother?"

"I'll let you figure that out. I'll give you a clue, however. Humans are the only living beings who, by their very nature, can access all levels. They alone can reflect God back to God."

Stunned, I leaned back in my chair, contemplating what the Seer had just said. "We provide a service to God? Now, *that's* an important responsibility!"

"Indeed it is. We can undertake serious work, if we are conscious. Work in service to the Highest Good. I'm glad you realize it."

She handed me the card and I examined it in detail.

"Okay," I said. "I think I'm ready to 'enter in' and 'read' the card."

She took the card back. "Actually, that would not be wise. At least not yet. This is a very powerful image, and one should not enter into it without a great deal of preparation."

I looked puzzled.

She continued, "You might get lost. Traditionally, Kabbalah wasn't taught to people until they were at least 40 and married. Oh—and male. We're no longer bound by those rules, but caution with this seemingly innocuous glyph is advisable. As I hope you've come to understand, it is a highly condensed description of many overlapping realities. It is important to be well grounded before 'moving up the ladder' so as not to go astray."

"I've been lost enough, recently. I don't want to go looking for trouble. Agreed. No 'entering in' to this card. Yet. But I have a question I've been meaning to ask on a different topic."

"Of course you do."

"When we were reading the blank card, and we both entered into a space of brilliant, pure light—and when my past-life self 'went through' the stone carving in the dolmen into a space filled with pure light—and when I climbed up Jacob's Ladder during my visit with Elen of the Ways into a place beyond words and separation—where did I go? Where did we go?"

"Where do you think we went?"

I spread my hands, unintentionally mimicking her now-familiar gesture. "I suppose somewhere above the lower levels of manifestation, maybe pretty close to the top."

"Possibly. But rather than trying to locate something in non-local reality, I could ask instead: What was your experience?"

"Compassion. Boundless love. Serenity. Peace."

"Perhaps we could call it God Consciousness? Higher Self? The Ground of Being? Unity Awareness?"

"Maybe so."

She recited, "We shall not cease from exploration/ And the end of all our exploring/ Will be to arrive where we started/ And know the place for the first time...."

"T.S. Eliot?"

"Yes. Now I'll ask you a question. Do you still think that all of this exists outside of you? Or are you beginning to realize that everything exists within, that you are an inseparable part of Oneness?"

I frowned, confused.

She tried again. "If Consciousness is everywhere, you are 'in' Consciousness and Consciousness is 'in' you. As the Sufi mystics say, 'God is as close to you as your jugular vein.' You are part of Awareness, of God Consciousness—pick your label. It is both imminent in you and transcendent beyond you. Just like Jacob's Ladder. You are like a wave in the ocean, rising and falling, inseparable even if you think you are a separate thing."

She placed the card back in the pile.

I closed my eyes, lost in this new contemplation. I felt buoyed by the Ocean, a part of it yet separate. I experienced for a moment a different reality, one where the particle and the wave merged, where I was separate yet united with the One. I felt completely at peace. After a moment or an eternity, the Seer's voice brought me back.

"I think we've done more than enough for one day. It's time for you to go home, ponder all you have learned, and practice. Remember: It's experience that matters, not the ideas you make up and not the stories you tell about it. Although, of course, we all tell stories. Telling stories, and listening to stories, makes life much more entertaining."

I stood up, gave the Seer a spontaneous bow of appreciation, and almost danced out the door. I turned back and saw the light had gone out.

Seven

A week later I returned. I entered the bookstore and knocked on the closet door. A voice called out, "Come in."

Everything looked just the same. In fact, nothing had changed, not even the Seer's clothes. She was still sitting at the mirror-top table, which was still covered with its mirage of cards; her black patent bag still dangled from the chair.

"I'm glad you are still here," I said, with an unexpected sense of relief.

She welcomed me with a smile. "You decided to return."

"I feel like I never left. Or rather, I feel like I was only gone for a moment."

"There is no time but now," she reminded me. "Then, looking at me quizzically, she asked, "Are you ready to begin?"

The cards appeared on the mirror-top table. I chose one or it chose me, and I began to 'read.'

✳

"Sorry—you have to stop a minute. I've got a cramp." The Scribe rubbed his aching hand and massaged his stubby fingers.

A gentle breeze ruffled the waters of the lake, carrying the subtle fragrance of dawn. Reassuringly, I said, "My story will soon be coming to an end."

The Scribe sighed. "I suppose it must, although I wish you could go on forever. But before you end, I have a question. You've talked about learning to 'read' the cards. What other techniques did you learn?"

"Ah, my friend, that would take another lifetime to describe, and I am lacking both time and strength." Seeing his disappointment, I relented. "In brief: I learned other ways to access the imaginal realms, and I gained confidence in moving through the veils that shield one reality from another. I learned to use Jacob's Ladder as a vehicle for exploring the inner, the outer, and the upper worlds. I learned—but dawn is almost upon us, and I need to finish my story."

With a start, the Scribe looked around and saw the faint tendrils of pink-tinged light spreading over the lake. He picked up his pen and nodded.

✴

I returned, returned again, and returned again and again to the Seer, each time receiving new teachings. I learned that sometimes we must become lost so that we can find our true selves. I learned that Now is the time—and the time is always Now. I learned that life is meaningful, but only you can determine the meaning of your life. I learned to trust the process of reflection and discernment—and that things are rarely what they seem. I learned to make Death my friend. The more I learned, the more mysterious and wonderful it all became, and the more I entered fully, joyfully, into life.

I began to ask fewer questions and need fewer answers. Or maybe I found my own answers. Gradually, my relationship with the Seer changed from teacher and pupil to mentor and junior colleague. I can't say we were friends, but we were friendly.

With time, the Seer appeared to become less substantial, almost as if she were retreating into another world.

Concerned about her fading appearance, I commented, "You are becoming a pale reflection of yourself. As if you are not quite here."

Slowly, she replied, "Maybe I never was, and it's just becoming more apparent. Or perhaps you are beginning to see more clearly."

And then she added, mysteriously, "'Now I see through a glass darkly, but then face to face….'" And then, even more mysteriously, "'What we call the beginning is often the end/ And to make an end is to make a beginning.'"

She looked at me with a soft and gentle gaze, her dark eyes fathomless. I met her gaze and looked through her eyes into Eternity.

From a faraway place, I heard her say, "When the time comes, and come it will, although there is only Now, remember The Library."

Eight

One day I returned and knocked on the door, but this time no voice called out, "Come in." Surprised, I turned the door handle and entered anyway.

No one was there, and the cards had vanished. Instead, there was a raven's feather and a folded note on the mirror-top table in front of the chair where the Seer always sat, where her black patent bag always dangled. I walked around the table, sat on her transparent Plexiglas chair, and picked up the feather. Slowly, I unfolded the note. It smelled of wild honey and lavender.

When you read this, I will have gone back to where I came from and from where I never completely left. I'm sure you will understand what I mean. We have accomplished our work together, and now it is time for you to continue the Work on your own.

I told you long ago (though the time is always Now), you had paid an initial instalment for these teachings, but the final price was still to be determined. Now is the time for me to tell you what you owe and how to honor your debt.

I charge you with the task of bringing this knowledge into your world to serve the Highest Good. Use the skills you have developed under my tutelage. How you choose to do so is up to you.

Suddenly, someone knocked hesitantly on the closet door. I folded the note and put it in my pocket. Someone knocked again.

My voice throaty with emotion, I called out, "Come in."

An anxious-looking young woman entered and looked around.

I gestured to the empty seat across from me, and she sat down nervously.

I began to draw cards out of the air with my fingers. The Hermit Tarot trump appeared, then a raven spirit-guide card, followed by the colorful Kabbalist Tree of Life diagram.

I glanced at my visitor and asked rhetorically, "Why be limited to working with only one deck?"

My visitor watched, mesmerized.

I raised my right hand again and, with a curious spiraling twist of my fingers, another card appeared and floated gently down through the air. The tabletop was soon covered with a kaleidoscope of cards of different designs, shapes, and sizes. I stirred the mirage with both hands and then looked at my visitor, my glance as piercing as a rook's.

"Now, what is your question?"

My visitor took a deep breath and prepared to speak.

I raised an imperious hand. "You don't have to tell me."

A clock ticked in the background, then stopped. My visitor turned to find the source of sound but there was none.

"The time is always now," I declared, and laughed. Then I shook myself, as if shaking off a chill. "Let's begin. Pick your first card."

My visitor reached forward, and a card moved toward her outstretched hand as if drawn by unseen attraction. She gave it to me, and I turned it over. I saw a volcano ringed with clouds, surrounded by water.

"If I were you, and this were *my* card," I began….

✳

My story told at last, the Scribe and I sit in companionable silence, like life-long friends who no longer need to use words to converse. The moon has set, and the pastel light of early dawn brightens the edges of the tranquil lake. Birds are starting to fluff their wings in the nearby trees, and I can hear the plop and splash of early-rising fish.

The Scribe puts down his ivory pen and closes his notebook. He stretches his arms over his head and pulls at his pendulous ears. A huge yawn spreads across his ample face.

"You were right," he says. "Your story was long—but only long enough. The time passed quickly." He places his hands together at heart level and bows to me.

I can hardly lift my hand to acknowledge his gesture. Suddenly I realize how weary to the bone and stiff I am. Stiff as a board. I lie without moving, reclining against the dune.

The Scribe sees my feeble efforts and asks, "Can I help?"

"Thank you. I think it's time for me to rest…."

"Would you like me to cover you with the blanket?"

I nod. Gently, he swaddles me in the sand-covered wrap. Then he sits beside me, opens his notebook, and takes out his pen. I close my eyes. My story told, I am now content to sleep, perhaps to dream.

✳

Word Associations, References, etc.

Card decks consulted for the readings include but are not limited to: The Wildwood Tarot, by Mark Ryan and John Matthews; the Rider Waite Tarot; The Dreampower Tarot, by R.J. Stewart; the Celtic Shaman's Pack, by John Matthews and Chesea Potter; and the Sacred Geometry Oracle Deck, by Francene Hart. However, none of the cards except for "The Burning Tower" correspond to any of these decks.

See Robert Moss's books *Active Dreaming, Sidewalk Tarot,* etc. Moss is a master storyteller and dreamworker. http://www.mossdreams.com

Rook—both a crow and a chess piece.

Mirage: to reflect, to look at (same root as mirror).

"If I were you, and this were my card…. "A phrase taken from Robert Moss's Lightning Dreamwork process. The central idea is that only the dreamer can know what the card means to them. Anyone else interpreting the dream is doing so from his or her own perspective—which can be very informative but is obviously not the same. To approach the dream or card reading "as if it were my dream/card" respects the integrity of all involved and can lead to many insights. See any of Moss's numerous publications on Active and Conscious Dreaming.

The raven is associated with the Morrigan, the shape-shifting Celtic goddess of death, Fate, and battle. She also is associated with rivers, fresh-water lakes, and waters.

The Ferryman: the Greek/Roman Charon/Kharon, who ferries the souls of the dead across the River Styx and demands a coin in payment; his dog ('Hound of Hell'), Cerberus.

"Some things are not meant to be understood by the mind but engaged with by the soul." Quote from *Walking with the Sin Eater,* by Ross Heaven, Llewellyn Publ., Woodbury, MN, 2010, p. 3.

"There is no future. There is only possibility." The philosopher Tim Freke at his Philosophical Deep Awake Retreat expressed these ideas about time. See *The Mystery Experience* and *Soul Story,* among other books. http://www.TimFreke.com

Merlin, gyrfalcon, and peregrine are types of raptors. Merlin also evokes Merlin the Magician. Peregrine is a word that means pilgrim. Maltese falcon refers to the movie about a valuable statue, a golden falcon painted black to disguise it. The eagle is a raptor; hence, "raptly alert."

"Turning and turning in the widening gyre/ The falcon cannot hear the falconer;/ Things fall apart; the center cannot hold…" W.B. Yeats, "The Second Coming."

Welsh tale of Math fab Mathonwy, told in the fourth branch of the medieval *Mabinogi* (also known as the *Mabinogion*) epic. It is the story of Blodeuwedd, Llew Llaw Gyffes, and Gronw Pebr. The *Mabinogi* was written in the 12th-13th centuries, but the stories are much older.

Arianrhod, medieval Welsh goddess of the moon and stars; transports souls to the other world. Oak, ash, and thorn, a trilogy of sacred trees in Celtic and Faery lore.

Yggdrasil: Nordic mythic World Tree that connects the nine worlds.

Psychopomp: one who leads souls to the Otherworld. Among others: the raven/Morrigan; the owl; Arianrhod.

Burning bush described in Exodus 3; burning bird that resurrects is the legendary phoenix in Greek mythology.

Gourd and staff: typical accouterments of medieval pilgrims; the scallop shell is the symbol of the pilgrimage to Santiago de Compostela in Spain. See *Following the Milky Way,* 2nd edition, by Elyn Aviva.

"Not all who wander are lost." A line from the poem "All that is gold does not glitter," written by J.R.R. Tolkien for *The Lord of the Rings.*

Well in the meadow: some of these images resonate with R.J. Stewart's work. See *Living Magical Arts* and *The Sphere of Art* series, and *The Underworld Initiation*, etc. http://www.rjstewart. org

Wake: to wake up; a wake as part of a festival gathering associated with death or a watching over the dead; or, something moving behind you, like the wake behind a ship.

C-shaped moon is in the waning phase.

Seven directions: four cardinal, plus up, down, and within.

"May the doors and gates…" Prayer of protection: see books by Robert Moss.

Hooded figure: resonates with The Hermit Tarot trump and with Merlin the Magician. The Salmon of Knowledge is found in Irish Celtic mythology.

The word "Abracadabra" is said to come from a Hebrew-Aramaic phrase that may mean, "I will create as I speak." The Aramaic inflection is probably closer to, "I create like the Word."

The Weaver goddesses, the Three Fates, and Spider Woman appear in different guises in mythology world-wide, including Greek, Nordic, Native American, and Asian traditions.

Chinese legend: In the Tang Dynasty, the weaving goddess floated down on a shaft of moonlight with her two attendants, and showed to the court official Guo Han in his garden that a goddess's robe is seamless for it is woven without the use of needle and thread, entirely on the loom. The phrase "a goddess's robe is seamless" became an idiom to express perfect workmanship.

"When Truth speaks through you…." Robert Moss.

Isis: Egyptian mother goddess, whose brother/husband was Osiris and whose falcon-headed son was Horus. Worship of Isis continued into Greco-Roman times and spread throughout the Roman Empire. She was worshipped as the Great Mother and goddess of health, magic, marriage, and wisdom.

Penelope: long-suffering wife of long-absent Odysseus, in Homer's *Odyssey.*

Beetle: a reference to the Egyptian dung beetle. Butterfly: ephemeral life. Poppies: opium dreams.

"A story is our shortest route to the meaning of things,..." Robert Moss, *Sidewalk Oracles.* New World Library, Novata, CA, 2015, p. 277.

Selkie: Scottish, Irish, and Faroese legendary creature that is a human that transforms into a seal—or perhaps vice versa. *The Secret of Roan Inish* is an excellent cinematic introduction.

A black mirror, also known as a magic or scrying mirror, is a divination tool. It is used to look into the past and see into the future. The obsidian scrying mirror of the Renaissance genius and esotericist Dr. John Dee is on display in the British Museum, London.

Elen Luyddog - Elen of the Hosts - is a well-known figure in Welsh legend. In the *Mabinogi,* she appears in the tale "Breuddwyd Macsen Wledig," in which she becomes the wife of the Emperor of Rome. Almost every 'Celtic' kingdom of Britain can trace its royal house back to Elen and Macsen, and Elen appears to have been influential in the early Christian church. Whether Elen was real is impossible to prove, but Macsen Wledig was a Roman emperor who lived in Wales. She is often confused with St. Helen, mother of Constantine.

Dream of a dark place where snakes slither and dogs roam: Temples of Asclepius contained such animals; people seeking healing went to the temples and underwent dream incubation practices. During their dreams, they hoped to receive healing or instructions on how to heal.

Oval drum: shaman's drum with reindeer-skin drumhead, used by indigenous Sami (Saami) people who live in the far north of Norway, Sweden, and Finland.

Jacob's Ladder: an image that links Earth and Heaven. It resonates both with the biblical and Kabbalist images of the Ladder. In Genesis 28:10-19, Jacob falls asleep and sees a stairway to Heaven, with angels traveling up and down, during his flight from his brother Esau. This is often called Jacob's Ladder.

Strange fruit hanging on a tree: resonates with the Norse god Odin who hung upside down on the tree, the Hanged Man Tarot card, and an American song about lynching African-Americans. "Strange Fruit" is a song performed most famously by Billie Holiday, who first sang and recorded it in 1939. Odin is a Norse Sky god associated with healing, death, war, knowledge, sorcery, poetry, and the runic alphabet.

"Reading the cards" technique of stepping into the frame: resonates with Robert Moss's teaching, among others.

Imaginal realm: "The imaginal realm is known in Islamic philosophy as *alam al-mithal,* the imaginal world. According to Avicenna, the imagination mediated between, and thus unified, human reason and divine being." (Wikipedia). See explications by Henry Corbin, Swedenborg, Coleridge, Carl Jung, Veronica Goodchild, among others.

"Notice the mystery...." Meditative prayer by spiritual teacher Terry Patton.

"Am I a man dreaming I was butterfly...": Concept taken from Zhuang Zhou, often known as Zhuangzi ("Master Zhuang"), an influential Chinese philosopher who lived around the 4th-century BCE.

"The pull of the Past, pulling my soul-stream...." Ideas about time and soul from Tim Freke.

"We enter an imaginal realm when we dream..." This discussion owes a great deal to Robert Moss's books and courses.

Dream of truck, told to author by Christine Coveney.

Indra's Net (also called Indra's jewels or Indra's pearls): The "Indra's Net" metaphor was developed by the Mahayana school in the 3rd-century *Avatamsaka Sutra.* It was further developed by the Chinese Buddhist Huayan school between the 6th and 8th centuries. It refers to the net of the Vedic god Indra, which hangs over his palace on Mount Meru, the axis mundi of Hindu cosmology. The net has a multifaceted jewel at each vertex, and each jewel is reflected in all of the other jewels. It is a graphic image of the interconnected universe.

The 17th-century Spanish writer Pedro Calderón de la Barca wrote a play entitled *Life is a Dream,* in which he allegorically explores topics including dream vs reality, and free will vs fate.

The Allegory of the Cave (also called the analogy of the cave, myth of the cave, metaphor of the cave, parable of the cave, and Plato's Cave) was presented by the Greek philosopher Plato in his work *The Republic* (514a–520a).

Dolmen on the hill: resonates with Cairn T in Loughcrew, an Irish megalithic complex also called Slieve na Caillaigh. Loughcrew is a collection of some 25 ruined dolmens or cairns, built on a hillside in County Meath. These dolmens or cairns are ancient megalithic (large-stone) structures, perhaps 5,000 years old, often originally covered by a large grassy mound. They had ritual and/or funereal functions.

Deer headdress: Archeological excavations at Star Carr in North Yorkshire, England, have uncovered at least 21, 10,000-year-old red-deer antler headdresses.

Honors the seven directions, etc.: adapted from R.J. Stewart's Inner Temples Inner Convocation practices, among other sources.

Philippians 4:7 English Standard Version (ESV) "…And the peace of God, which surpasses all understanding…."

Tiresias: a Greek mythological figure. Tiresias was a blind Theban prophet of Apollo, famous for clairvoyance—and for being transformed into a woman for seven years. In one version, after either Hera or Athena blinded him, he was given the gift of seeing the future. Isaac the Blind: an important medieval Kabbalist from Provence, France. His nickname was "of much Light," meaning to have excellent eyesight. This appears to have been ironic or a coded way of referring to his having inner vision. Isaac named the ten Sefirot on the Tree of Life and first adopted the idea of metempsychosis (transmigration of the soul). Odin: see earlier reference.

The Library: a classic telesm or well-established imaginal "form" or "location," visited in a number of esoteric traditions. The 20th-century Argentine writer Jorge Luis Borges wrote a short story called "The Library of Babel," in which he conceives of the universe as a peculiar kind of library.

Jacob's Ladder explanation is based on the writings of Z'ev ben Shimon Halevi and of Maggy Whitehouse. http://www.kabbalahsociety.org/

See, among many others, Jude Currivan, *The Cosmic Hologram – In-formation at the Center of Creation*; and Ervin Laszlo, *The Intelligence of the Universe*.

See R.J. Stewart's "Stillness Meditation," http://www.rjstewart.org

"We shall not cease from exploration..." From "Little Gidding," by T.S. Eliot.

"I return, return again, and return again and again" references the song, "Return Again," composed by Shlomo Carlbach.

1 Corinthians 13:12, King James Version: "For now we see through a glass, darkly; but then face to face: now I know in part; but then shall I know even as also I am known."

"'What we call the beginning is often the end....' From "Little Gidding," by T.S. Eliot.

"To sleep, perchance to dream..." Shakespeare, Hamlet's soliloquy, III, I, 65-68.

Index

L

Lao-tzu 130
Library 144, 145, 149, 152, 153, 156, 158, 172, 184
Library Card 144
Lleu Llaw Gyffes 15

M

Mabinogi 179, 181
Macsen Wledig 59, 181
Mahabharata 150
Math 15, 179
mirror 5, 22, 31, 44, 54, 55, 57, 72, 73, 80, 82, 94, 107, 129, 164, 169, 170, 173, 178, 181
Morrigan 11, 178, 179
Moss, Robert v, 178, 180, 182

N

Nachmanides 143

O

Odin 86, 142, 182, 184
Osiris 180

P

past life 138, 142, 143
Patton, Terry 182
Phoenix 28
pilgrim 29, 179
pilgrimage 125, 179
psychopomp 11, 23, 54

R

raven 7, 8, 9, 12, 23, 96, 97, 114, 157, 173, 174, 178, 179
Raven Card 7
References 178
runes 4, 88

S

salmon 35, 36, 37
seal 50, 51, 52, 53, 54, 181
Sefirah 75, 76, 148
Sefirot 75, 76, 77, 148, 156, 183
Selkie 53, 181
Shakespeare 151, 184
Socrates 130, 151
soul v, 11, 19, 110, 139-143, 151, 157, 178, 182, 184
soul-stream 110, 139, 151, 157, 182
spider-woman 42, 159
Stewart, R.J. v, 178, 180, 183

Elyn Aviva is a transformational traveler, writer, and fiber artist. Currently living in Oviedo (Asturias), Spain, she has a life-long interest in pilgrimage, earth mysteries, the Western Esoteric Tradition, and Kabbalah. Her Ph.D. in anthropology was on walking the modern Camino de Santiago across Spain. She also has an M.Div. degree (Iliff School of Theology). Aviva is author of a number of articles, travel narratives, and novels, including *Following the Milky Way* and *The Journey - A Novel of Spiritual Quest.* She is also co-author with her husband, Gary White, of the "Powerful Places Guidebooks" series.

To learn more, go to www.pilgrimsprocess.com and Elyn's Facebook page, Elyn Aviva Writes. To learn about Elyn's fiber art, go to www.fiberalchemy.com.

Lightning Source UK Ltd.
Milton Keynes UK
UKHW01f1513160618
324343UK00001B/63/P